W9-BIY-682

JUN 2009

BAYOU JUDGMENT

This Large Print Book carries the
Seal of Approval of N.A.V.H.

BAYOU JUDGMENT

ROBIN CAROLL

THORNDIKE PRESS
A part of Gale, Cengage Learning

Detroit • New York • San Francisco • New Haven, Conn • Waterville, Maine • London

GALE
CENGAGE Learning™

Copyright © 2008 by Robin Miller.
Thorndike Press, a part of Gale, Cengage Learning.

ALL RIGHTS RESERVED
This is a work of fiction. Names, characters, places, and incidents are either the product of the author's imagination or are used fictitiously, and any resemblance to actual persons, living or dead, business establishments, events, or locales is entirely coincidental.
Thorndike Press® Large Print Christian Mystery.
The text of this Large Print edition is unabridged.
Other aspects of the book may vary from the original edition.
Set in 16 pt. Plantin.
Printed on permanent paper.

LIBRARY OF CONGRESS CATALOGING-IN-PUBLICATION DATA

Caroll, Robin.
    Bayou judgment / by Robin Caroll. — Large print ed.
      p. cm. — (Thorndike large print Christian mystery)
    Originally published: New York : Harlequin, 2008.
    ISBN-13: 978-1-4104-1487-8 (alk. paper)
    ISBN-10: 1-4104-1487-6 (alk. paper)
    1. Murder—Fiction. 2. Louisiana—Fiction. 3. Large type
books. I. Title.
PS3603.A7673B38 2009
813'.6—dc22   2009001705

Published in 2009 by arrangement with Harlequin Books S.A.

Printed in the United States of America
1 2 3 4 5 6 7 13 12 11 10 09

Forgive and act; deal with each man according to all he does, since you know his heart (for you alone know the hearts of all men.)

— *1 Kings* 8:39

To Krystina Danyelle Harden,
Because you inspire me.
Love, Aunt Robin

ACKNOWLEDGMENTS

My deepest gratitude to my editor, Krista Stroever, who continues to teach me and make my books be the best they can; and my agent, Kelly Mortimer, for being my constant cheerleader.

Huge thanks and love to my mentor, Colleen Coble — you rock!

Heartfelt thanks to my family and friends for invaluable input, love and support: BB, Camy, Cheryl, Dineen, Heather, Lisa, Pammer, Ron, Ronie and Trace.

Sincere appreciation to my family for continued encouragement and support — Mom, Papa, Bek, Bubba, Robert, Connie and Willie.

Humble thanks to my prayer group — words are not enough. Love y'all!

To my daughters — Emily, Remington and Isabella — who allow me time to write. I love you SO much!

My most genuine gratitude to my husband, Case, for his love, support and encouragement that allow me to do what I so love. Love Always, Me.

All glory to my Lord and Savior, Jesus Christ.

ONE

"You don't really want to hurt anyone. Please, let's talk about this." Felicia Trahan wrapped the phone cord around her finger and didn't uncoil it until the tip turned white.

Pastor Spencer Bertrand stood beside Felicia's desk, listening to her side of the conversation while he gazed over the crisis center. Every operator hunched over their desk, speaking in low tones. There'd been so many callers today, people with problems. He wanted to help them all, but knew it impossible, even given the slow pace of the day. He glanced at the clock on the wall — 7:00 p.m.

Father God, please touch these people's hearts. Help them. Bless them.

He refocused on Felicia. A silver-handled cane leaned against the side of the desk. Already graduated to a cane — he had to admire her tenacity. A little under a year

11

ago she'd had surgery to give her use of her left leg. Some people with cerebral palsy weren't so fortunate. Or wealthy enough to afford new procedures.

She glanced up, her startling blue eyes wide. Heat tickled the back of his neck. Although well-trained, the counselors sometimes had to pass a caller off to him. That Felicia had waved him over said a lot. She requested his assistance less than any other operator. If she wanted his help, the situation must be dire.

He didn't know if he could muster enough energy to play the part he'd projected himself to play. Fake. Phony. When it came right down to it, that's all he was.

"I understand. Listen, Pastor Spence is here now if you'd like to talk with him. He's a wonderful adviser in matters such as these." Felicia's soft voice could charm anyone. "Of course, I understand. But I think it would be bene—"

Her lips pressed together. She stared at him, holding up a finger. The intensity of her gaze made him uncomfortable. He sat on the edge of her desk, all too aware of the close proximity.

"Are you sure? Because he's really g—" She shook her head. "Okay. Can I at least get your name? If you call again, you can ask for me." She grabbed her pen, poising it over the call log. Some counselors doodled while talking, but not Felicia.

"Thanks, Winnie. I hope you'll call me back." She jerked the headset free and tossed it on the desk. "That was a live one, Spence."

He crossed his arms over his chest. "What's the deal?"

"Young woman, early twenties, I'd guess, got dumped by her fiancé several months ago because he'd found someone new."

"Common this time of year. More break-ups during Mardi Gras than at Christmas."

"I know. But this woman has some serious hostility eating at her."

He straightened. "Such as?"

"She says she's entertaining thoughts of hurting the new girlfriend. Physically hurting her."

"Did she sound like someone just trying to get attention or mess with the center?" That happened quite often, people calling in with outlandish prank complaints.

"No. She sounded serious." Felicia shivered. "And determined."

"Did she give you any details?"

"Just her name. Winnie." She stood, flexing her left hand, which had also recently been operated on.

"That she called us is a cry for help. Maybe she'll call back."

"I hope so." She smiled that barely there smile of hers.

His heart pounded before he could will it to behave. No matter how perfect she seemed, Felicia Trahan was now, and always would be, off limits to the likes of him.

The phone rang.

When she lifted the receiver, Spencer made fast tracks to his office. Just being in Felicia's presence made pinpricks jab his conscience.

Father God, please help me. You know what a sinner I am, and I'm just trying to follow Your guidance. I can't be attracted to someone so sweet, so pure . . . not when I'm such a mess.

Spencer cradled his head in his hands, his elbows digging into the ratty wooden desk. His mug sat half empty, but the smell hovering over the coffeepot in the corner didn't entice him to get a fresh cup. He glanced at the notes on his desk calendar. Monday morning he'd have to visit Jon Garrison. A monthly visit he'd rather walk through fire to avoid. Hadn't he paid enough already?

Felicia stood in the break room, staring out the window of the Vermilion Parish Christian Crisis Center — VPCCC, for short.

Someone had spilled bright purple, emerald-green and fool's gold over Lagniappe, Louisiana.

Comedy/tragedy masks decorated every light post along the town square, mocking pedestrians. Purple-and-gold beads draped the moonlit storefronts and doorways, casting a sparkling array of color prisms into the shroud of darkness.

"Welcome to Mardi Gras madness." Jolie Landry, Felicia's best friend and roommate, chuckled.

Felicia smiled. "Is the center always this bad during Mardi Gras season?" She'd only been working at the center for a few months, while Jolie had been with it since its inception a little more than a year ago.

"Pretty much. Spence says it'll die down once Ash Wednesday arrives."

At the mention of their boss's name, Felicia's stomach lurched. Why did the man tie her in knots? She'd sworn off men permanently after losing Frank. The human heart was too fragile a thing, a lesson she wouldn't forget.

Jolie continued, not noticing Felicia's silence. "All I can say is, thank goodness it's Friday."

"Yeah. Uh, Jo, Wesley phoned the apartment several times before I left, begging me

15

to talk you into returning his calls."

Running a hand through her strawberry-blond hair, Jolie shrugged. "I don't think I'm ready just yet."

"He says he can explain everything about Sadie."

Sadie Thompson, the woman who made her way through the men in Lagniappe, one poor sap at a time.

Jolie let out a sigh. "What do you think?"

"I think you should hear him out. It could all be a horrible misunderstanding."

"But . . . Sadie?"

"Come on, a woman calls here, refuses to give her name, and tells you Sadie's been seen with your boyfriend . . sounds iffy to me, yes?"

"But he confirmed it was true." Jolie's pretty smile turned into a pout.

"And it's exactly why I think you owe it to Wesley to let him explain."

"Hmm." Before Jolie could say more, her cell chirped. She flipped open the phone. "Hello."

Probably Wesley, begging for a second chance. Felicia smiled. Although they'd only been dating three months, he doted on Jolie. The anonymous caller to the center had only been trying to stir up trouble.

"No, Kipp, I won't."

Felicia jerked her attention to Jolie. Not Wesley, but Jolie's brother.

"I told you what to do. I don't care what they're threatening. . . ."

Uh-oh. Didn't sound good. Kipp's gambling debts had piled up. Lately, he'd been calling Jolie constantly for money. Said some bad guys were calling in their markers. Using bats, if it came to that. And there had been that article in the paper about the hospitalization of several men who'd owed some freelancers money.

"Look, I'm about to leave. I'll run home and change clothes, then meet you at Fisherman's Wharf at eight. You'd better be there, Kipp." Jolie slipped the phone back into its belt clip.

"You're going to meet him?" Why couldn't Jolie see her brother spelled bad news?

"He says they're threatening *me* now."

Threatening her — Jolie? Felicia shook her head. "Do you think that's a good idea? Meeting him, I mean?" Little pricks of foreboding poked against her subconscious. She'd heard rumors that the police were cracking down on gambling loan sharks due to the death of several people who'd owed them money. Now they were threatening Jolie?

"I'm the only family he has left." Jolie's

pretty face twisted with painful memories. "Well, aside from Uncle Roger and Martin. But since they're in . . ." Jolie squeezed Felicia's shoulder. "I'm so sorry."

"Not your fault. We've all been hurt, yes?" Felicia blinked back hot tears. Don't remember the diamond solitaire sitting alone in the jewelry box back at the apartment. Don't let the grief beat her down.

"I just feel awful."

Felicia smiled, despite the pain twisting her heart. "You can't control other people's actions, Jo. Anyway —" she brushed away the few tears that had escaped "— you can't control Kipp, either."

"I have to convince him to go to the police. This situation has gone from bad to worse. If he doesn't go, I will."

"Good for you. Especially since they threatened you." Just the idea gave Felicia the heebie-jeebies.

Jolie's laugh was flat and humorless. "So Kipp says. They probably don't even know I exist. He's just trying to extort me into getting the money from you."

"I'll gladly give you whatever you need. You know that, yes?"

"I know you would, but I can't keep taking your money to get him out of trouble. Kipp has to learn to take responsibility for

18

his gambling addiction." Jolie didn't look convinced. "He can't keep having someone bail him out."

"True."

Glancing at the clock, Jolie grabbed her purse. "Oh, man, look at the time. Almost seven-thirty already. I gotta split if I'm gonna have time to change before heading to the Wharf." She gave Felicia a quick hug. "Pray for me, okay?"

"Always." She grabbed Jolie's hand. "Do me a favor and give Wesley a break. He says there's a perfectly logical reason he met with Sadie. Call him, yes?"

"I will."

"He's a good man, Jo."

Jolie's soft smile flashed before she grabbed another hug. "*Merci* for everything. I love ya."

"Ditto."

Felicia leaned heavily on her cane as she returned to her desk. Phones rang as she slipped into the chair. By the sound of things, a long night awaited her.

"I don't know what else to do, Felicia." Wesley Ellender's voice cracked over the connection.

Felicia gripped her cell phone tighter. "She called me from her cell not twenty

19

minutes ago. She was on her way home." Jolie should've been there already. Something wasn't right.

"I know. She told me to pick her up at the apartment." He sighed. "Maybe she intended to stand me up. Make me pay for the whole Sadie thing."

"That's not like Jolie. She told me y'all were having a late supper." Where could Jolie have gone? Long tendrils of unease coiled in Felicia's chest.

"I'm getting worried. Her car is here, but she's not answering the door. I can't hear the TV or radio, either. You know how she likes her music."

Very true. Jolie loved listening to contemporary Christian music at full volume. So loudly several neighbors had complained about the noise.

The worry spread to Felicia's stomach. She glanced around the center at the other operators. Surely one of them would give her a ride to the apartment. She didn't want to wait for her driver. "I'll get there as quickly as I can."

She grabbed her cane and headed to Spence's office. As her boss, he needed to know she had to run home. He'd created a family-type working atmosphere — people could have time off for personal or family

20

reasons, personal calls weren't taboo and he never turned down someone asking him for help. A perfect boss.

All the more reason for her to stay focused on the business at hand.

His office door sat ajar. He held his head in his hands, his face down. Praying? A lot of people might have a problem with their preacher being so young, having unruly hair and a tattoo on his finger — which Felicia had just recently noticed — but Spence's congregation loved him. These things made him seem more approachable, maybe. Felicia cleared her throat and tapped on the door. "Spence?"

He jerked his attention to her. "Yes? Did Winnie call back?"

"Who? Oh, no. It's about Jolie. She's supposed to be home, her car is there, but she isn't answering the door. I've tried calling the house and her cell, and can't get an answer. I need to find someone to run me to the apartment to check on her."

Shoving to his feet, he scooped his keys from the desk. "Let's go. I'll tell Michael to watch things here."

"I can get one of the girls to take me."

"Don't be silly. I'll drive you."

She wet her lips. He made perfect sense. Then again, he didn't know how easily he affected her. "Okay."

Spence told his assistant they'd be back shortly, escorted Felicia to his car and steered toward the apartment complex just down the street. He glanced between the road and her face. "It's probably nothing."

Maybe she was making an ocean out of a bayou, but Felicia sensed something amiss. Terribly wrong. "Maybe. But she could've fallen in the bathroom and hit her head or something. She'd been in a hurry."

He didn't respond, just continued driving.

Felicia took her house key from her purse, clutching the cold metal in her palm. This wasn't like Jolie. Even mad, she wouldn't avoid Felicia. Jolie would have answered the phone when she saw the center's number on the caller ID. If she'd been able.

Sucking in air, Felicia silently prayed.

What had happened? Had someone picked Jolie up from the apartment? Nothing made sense. The ten-minute drive dragged out to an eternity, each turn of the tires as slow as a debutante's descent on the stairs. Jolie could be passed out on the floor right now, waiting for help.

Felicia tightened her fist over the key. Her nails dug into her palm, but the sinking feeling didn't leave the pit of her stomach.

Spence parked in the spot next to Jolie's

car. Wesley paced curbside. He rushed to help Felicia. "I've been pounding on the door and calling her name. Nothing." Deep lines dug across his forehead into his handsome features.

Felicia moved as fast as she could. She dropped the key. Wesley, a regular Johnny-on-the-spot, handed it to her. She jabbed the key at the slot several times. Sweat slicked her palms.

"Here, allow me." Spence took the key from her and slipped it into the lock, twisting the knob. He stepped over the threshold.

A strange coppery smell hung in the air. Felicia swallowed hard. "Jolie? Jo, are you here?"

Silence hung over the apartment like an ominous cloud.

Wesley passed Felicia in the foyer, striding to the living room.

"Oh, sweet mercy, no!"

What? Felicia hobbled toward the sound of Wesley's wails, only to have Spence step in front of her, blocking her path. She could barely make out Wes kneeling on the floor.

"You don't want to see this." Spence drew his muscular arms around her, turning her in the direction of the kitchen. "Where's your phone?"

She stiffened in his embrace. "What is it?

Is it Jolie?"

"We need to call 911. Where's your phone?" He kept maneuvering her away from the living room.

"There's an extension in the kitchen. She needs an ambulance?"

"No, *sha,* not an ambulance. We need the police."

"Police? For what?"

"Jolie's been murdered."

Two

How could she have failed Jolie so badly?

Felicia stared at the kitchen table, shredding tissues with trembling hands. Jolie had been her best friend. The grief would come, she knew from experience, but for now, guilt battered into her. It'd been her job to take care of Jolie, and she'd failed miserably.

"Felicia?" Sheriff Bubba Theriot limped into the kitchen, the badge on his chest glaring under the bright fluorescent lights. "I need to ask you a few questions."

Raw emotions knotted into a lump in the back of her throat. She forced a cough. "Please, have a seat."

He lowered himself into the chair next to her and ran a hand through his auburn hair. "I called Luc for you. He's on his way."

"Merci." She glanced over his shoulder to the foyer. She couldn't see Spence amid the tangle of uniformed men. Where could he be? An uncanny need to see him gripped

her. He provided her with a strong sense of security. Stability. Hope.

"I need to ask you about tonight." The sheriff whipped out a small notebook from his front pocket.

She fisted the shredded tissues into a tight ball and breathed deeply.

"Can you walk me through all your contact with Jolie this evening?"

She licked her lips. "I arrived at the center around six or so, half an hour before my shift." She ran a finger along the silver-handled cane. "I always allow a little extra time before I'm supposed to plug into the phones."

"I can understand." The sheriff's eyes softened behind his glasses. He, too, had to endure grueling physical therapy to get his life back after an attack last year. She knew — she'd seen him at the clinic several times.

"Jolie greeted me like normal, as soon as I came in."

The sheriff wrote on his notepad, head bent. "Did you notice anything unusual about her attitude or frame of mind? Had anything happened lately that'd upset her?"

"I suppose. She and her boyfriend had a spat two nights ago. He'd been trying to get her to talk to him, to let him explain. He'd called the apartment several times today,

26

asking me to talk to her on his behalf."

"That would be Wesley Ellender, yes?"

"Yes. They've been dating exclusively for about three months, I'd guess."

"Do you know what they argued about?"

While the details would come out — Wesley would surely explain everything to the police — Felicia hated to repeat rumors. But someone had murdered her friend. She couldn't hold back on anything that might be important. "Somebody told Jolie they saw Wes with Sadie."

"Sadie Thompson?"

Felicia nodded. "Jolie got upset. She avoided his calls and wouldn't answer the door when he came by."

"So, he asked you to plead his case for him?"

"Not exactly." Though Wes's voice *had* taken on a whining tone. "He just told me there was an explanation and asked if I could try to get Jolie to at least hear him out."

"Uh-huh." The sheriff scribbled the pen against the paper. "So, you told her he'd called?"

"Yes. I asked her to listen to him. Give him a chance."

"Why?"

"Why, what?"

"Why would you advise her to listen to him?"

Felicia glanced around the kitchen. If she sat still enough, quietly enough, she could almost hear Jolie's laughter as they concocted something on the stove. Felicia the teacher, Jolie the student. The memories assaulted Felicia, a lingering and constant reminder that she had failed to protect her friend. She knew it'd never be all right again. She couldn't bring Jolie back.

But she could make sure her killer was caught and brought to justice.

"Felicia?"

She darted her gaze back to the sheriff's face. Right, get back on track. Don't let her emotions control her. Focus on Jolie and Wesley. "They were happy before. Then some woman called Jolie at the center and told her that she'd seen Wesley with Sadie. When Jolie asked Wesley, he said he'd met with Sadie, but could explain the circumstances. Jolie was too hurt at the time." Felicia gave a soft sigh. "I thought it'd all been a misunderstanding, and she should at least give him the chance to explain. Happiness in romance doesn't come around every day, Sheriff. When you have something special, you should fight to protect it."

His expression became tender. "I understand." He cleared his throat. "What'd she say?"

"That she would call him."

"Anything else?"

Felicia told the sheriff about Kipp's situation.

He stopped writing notes when she mentioned the loan sharks. "Did she give you a name?"

"No. I don't think Kipp told her." She tossed the tissue ball on the table. "She did tell me Kipp said they threatened her if he didn't pay up."

More scribbling in the notebook. "Was she frightened?"

"Not really. She implied Kipp might be making that up just to get her to give him the money."

"Did Jolie happen to mention how much money he owed?"

Felicia shrugged. "She never really said, for sure, but indicated it was several thousand dollars."

"She was a single gal, working at the center for low wages — how would she have that kind of money?"

"She doesn't . . . didn't. But I do." Her heart twisted.

"Why wouldn't Kipp just come to you?"

"I don't know. I guess he knew if *she*

asked me, I'd gladly give her money. I didn't know him very well, didn't approve of his methods. I wouldn't have given the money to him, but I would've to Jolie. I've done it before." She blinked back tears. "I'd have paid anything to keep Jolie safe."

"She didn't want to give him the money?"

"No. She wanted him to go to the police. Report these loan sharks."

"He didn't want to?"

"I don't know for certain, but it's my guess he wouldn't."

"Anything else?"

Her shoulders tensed, and she wanted to cringe. The beginnings of a headache pounded behind her eyes. "Around eight-forty-five, Wes called me at the center. Jolie was supposed to meet him for supper at the Crawfish Café at eight-thirty. She never showed."

"Why'd he call you?"

"He didn't know about the meeting with Kipp. He thought she might still be at the center, talking to me." Aspirin — she needed something for the pulsating at her temples.

"Uh-huh." Sheriff Theriot flipped the page in his notebook, the sound drowning out the hum of activity in the living room.

"I called Jolie on her cell. She answered on the second ring. She said she was running late from meeting with Kipp and planned to have supper with Wes." Felicia glanced at the clock — 3:10, no wonder exhaustion dragged at her. She blinked, forcing herself to focus. "I told her Wes was looking for her. She said she'd call and tell him to pick her up at the apartment."

More writing. "And then what?"

The lump in her chest crept slowly up to stick at the base of her throat. "I told her I was proud of her. For meeting with Wes, hearing him out. She told me she loved me and hung up." Just when she thought she'd stifled her pain, Felicia found tears on her face. "I never heard from her again."

He wanted to check on Felicia. No, he *needed* to, but Deputy Gary Anderson persisted with his questions. Spencer glanced around the small living room. A sofa, coffee table, chair with ottoman and TV on a stand. Simple furnishings. Jolie's body had been removed, but the blood and the tape outline remained, a chilling visual of the crime. How would Felicia ever be able to stay in this apartment again? She'd probably move back home with her mother and brother. It would be for the best.

"Pastor Bertrand, c—"

"Spencer. Please, call me Spencer or

Spence."

The deputy smiled. "Spencer, can you tell me about your contact with Ms. Landry this evening?"

He walked the deputy through his limited contact with Jolie tonight while Deputy Anderson made notes in a little spiral notebook.

"Now, tell me about the center."

"We take calls from anyone having emotional or spiritual problems. Our counselors advise accordingly, but if anyone feels they can't handle a person's issues, they pass the call to me."

"Bet you get a lot of weird ones."

"We get our fair share."

"Any that cross the line?"

"Sometimes." Where was the good deputy heading with this line of questioning?

"Did Ms. Landry take any of those type calls?"

"Not that I'm aware of."

"Nobody she had to pass off to you?"

"Not lately."

"Mmm." Deputy Anderson looked up from his notebook. "Have there been any threats against any of the counselors?"

"A time or two. Normally an abusive husband who's mad because we advise the battered wife to seek help at a women's shelter."

"Recently?"

"No."

"Maybe no one told you?"

Spencer shook his head. "Those situations are immediately brought to my attention."

"I see."

But he didn't. Nobody understood what it took out of Spencer each time he had to handle one of those calls. Memories resurfaced, ones that kept him awake in the middle of the night.

"I think that's about it for now. The sheriff will have more questions for you tomorrow. We'll need you to come by the station in the morning and give an official statement."

Spencer nodded, but his heart raced. He knew the routine only too well. "Did you find the murder weapon?"

"We're looking." Deputy Anderson shoved to his feet and passed Spencer a business card. "If you think of anything else, give us a call."

"Will do." But he wouldn't.

He'd avoid the police as much as possible. He had too much to lose — experience had taught him that.

Felicia crammed clothes into her suitcase. In his commanding way, her brother Luc had shown up and ordered her to pack. He'd take her back to the Trahan home.

How long until she could come back? Would she ever be able to return without memories and pain? Luc's tone implied she wouldn't be returning. Not with a killer on the loose.

But she would.

The apartment was her home now. She wouldn't allow some murderer to send her running away with her tail between her legs. Felicia dropped to the bed, her emotions warring within. She'd fought too hard to move out on her own, gain some sense of independence. Be in a position to help someone. That person had been Jolie, and look what had happened.

Even though she'd known Jolie for years, after the incident that had robbed Felicia of Frank, the two had bonded, despite all odds. Jolie, related to the men who'd killed Frank; Felicia, fiancée of the victim. But the two women had forged a relationship built on the shared grief of loss.

Why hadn't she begged Jolie not to meet Kipp? In her heart of hearts, Felicia felt certain whoever had killed her best friend was connected to the people Kipp owed money to. They'd probably followed him, seen him with Jolie, then exacted their revenge. Jolie had been murdered. While she hadn't been able to save Jolie, Felicia would do whatever it took to find her killer.

A soft knock on the bedroom door interrupted her thoughts.

"*Boo*? Ready to go?" Luc hovered in the doorway, his presence reassuring but authoritative. Her protector. She appreciated his support, but resented that he was not able to comprehend her need to stand on her own two feet.

Well, not really. She grabbed her cane. Not yet, but soon.

Luc lifted her suitcase with one hand and gripped her elbow with the other, leading her down the hall to the front door. They passed two officers talking with Wes in the little sitting area.

She should look away, she knew, but couldn't resist a glance in the living room as they headed out the front door.

The blood, now a deep brown, stained the floor.

Felicia's gagging reflex activated. She jerked free of Luc's hold and hobbled to the front door, cane tapping against the floor. She needed cool air.

The hint of honeysuckle blended with the early-blooming azaleas, filling the predawn air with sweetness. Too syrupy. Leaning over the sidewalk, Felicia lost her supper behind the box hedges.

A gentle hand pulled back her hair.

She straightened and wiped her mouth with the back of her good hand. Her gaze met Spence's.

"It's okay." His voice came out soft.

She gave a shaky smile.

"You okay?" Luc moved to join them.

"Oh, Ms. Trahan, I'm so sorry for what happened." Mr. McRae waddled across the walkway. Her landlord patted her shoulder, his pudgy face wreathed in concern. "Don't you worry about a thing. I'll get the apartment cleaned up for you."

"You don't have to do that," she muttered.

"I don't think she'll be coming back, Mr. McRae." Luc hovered at her side.

"Oh." Her landlord's eyes held such sadness as he looked at Felicia. "I'll be sorry to see you go, but I understand."

Back that truck up. She might be grief stricken, but she did still have a voice. "Actually, Mr. McRae, I'd like to stay."

Luc took hold of her elbow. "You aren't thinking clearly, *Boo.* You can't come back here."

She locked stares with Mr. McRae. "Could I change apartments? I'd still need one on the bottom floor, of course."

"Certainly. Six-A left last week. I finished the paint job just this morning."

"Felicia," Luc interrupted, "I don't think this is a good idea. Why don't you take a couple of days to consider your opt—"

"No." She shook her head to emphasize. "I'm not moving back home. Mr. McRae, how soon could I move into the new apartment?"

"By the end of next week." He glanced at Luc and must have seen the storm clouds brewing in her brother's face. "But maybe you should think about this."

"My decision is made. I'll arrange to have my things moved next weekend, after I see about packing up J-Jolie's things." She hated how her voice cracked merely saying her name.

As if it were the most natural gesture in the world, Spence took a step closer to her.

Before anyone could argue, a uniformed officer ran up the walkway. "Sheriff, we have a neighbor who has some information you might want to hear."

Sheriff Theriot scooted from the doorway. "Whatcha got, Alan?"

Felicia took two steps to get closer to the policeman, and craned to listen.

"Next-door lady says she heard a woman pounding on the door here around seven-forty-five. Says she looked out her window and saw the woman, can identify her. Ms. Landry must have let her inside because the neighbor says she heard all kinds of yelling and screaming."

Felicia's heartbeat drowned out coherent thought. Jolie yelling? Never. Jolie's nature wouldn't allow her to raise her voice.

"Does she know the woman?" Sheriff Theriot asked.

"Yeah. Says she recognized the woman as Sadie Thompson."

"I'm on my way." The sheriff turned to Felicia. "Remember, I'll need you to come by the station in the morning to give your official statement." His gaze drifted to her brother. "We'll get to the bottom of it, Luc."

But Felicia paid no attention as she let Luc lead her to his SUV. Why would Sadie come to the apartment?

And what would possess Jolie to let her in?

THREE

Sweat dripped into Felicia's eyes.

"*Allons,* girl, you can do it." Her physical therapist, Mark, shoved her through the last set of leg presses. "If you want to walk without that cane, you haveta finish this."

Flashing him a stabbing look, Felicia grunted and completed the set. She let out a long sigh and wiped her brow with a towel. "Shouldn't this be getting easier after all these months?"

Mark chuckled. "We're working new muscles."

"You're a slave driver."

"But you love me." He grinned and waggled his eyebrows.

Despite her exhaustion, she smiled back. He had her there — she did adore him. He knew her goal of walking without aid and pushed her hard to achieve it. Besides that, he was a good person. Nice. Honest. A person she could allow herself to care about without worrying about romantic entanglements. Mark had a sweet wife waiting on him at home. No threat.

"Are you sure you don't want to take a couple of days to get over the incident? You can do your exercises at home."

The incident? What a polite way to say her friend had been murdered.

"No. Jolie wouldn't have wanted me to cut back on her account. She wanted to see me walk alone."

"I'm sorry. I didn't mean to upset you." Mark laid a comforting hand on her shoulder.

"It's okay." She wiped her face. "I think I'll go hit the showers now."

"Luc picking you up?"

"Or the driver." Pressing hard on the cane, she shoved herself to her feet. Her leg muscles, unused for a lifetime, quaked under her weight.

"I'll see you tomorrow, then." Mark gave a mock punch to her upper arm. "You done good today, girl."

"*Merci.*" Her thoughts jumbled as she lumbered to the locker room.

Three days after the *incident,* and the police still hadn't found the murder weapon. Meanwhile, they were looking for Sadie Thompson to question her, as well as Kipp

40

Landry, who seemed to have fallen off the face of the earth.

Felicia stiffened her back. Her best friend's murderer walked around free as a bird. No, this wouldn't do. If the police didn't get answers soon, maybe she'd do a little probing herself. She owed it to Jolie.

An hour and a shower later, she had no further revelation on the matter. The hot spray had eased some of the tightness in her left calf, but the ache grew, creeping up into her thigh. She hobbled back into the lobby of the physical therapy center.

"Hey, can I give you a lift?" asked CoCo, Luc's girlfriend.

Felicia smiled. "You didn't have to come fetch me, yes?"

"Don't be silly. I wanted to check on you." CoCo hugged her. "*Allons,* let's blow this joint."

Felicia had to laugh at her friend's gangster imitation. She followed CoCo to the Jeep, her steps slower than normal.

"Luc told me you didn't plan on staying at home." CoCo turned over the engine and headed toward the Trahan house.

Ah, so that's why he sent CoCo to pick her up — in hopes his girlfriend could talk her out of staying at the apartment complex.

She hated to disappoint her big brother,

but Felicia had no intention of staying back at home. "Yep. I need to arrange to move my things into the new apartment this weekend."

CoCo shot her a quick glance before shifting her attention back to the road. "Do you think that's wise?"

Felicia bit back the retort, the one yelling *this is my life and I'll do whatever I want.* CoCo loved her and was concerned for her. Felicia couldn't blame her, really. For years, Felicia had been the stabilizing influence on the Trahan family, a job she'd never applied for but had just naturally stepped into after the death of her grandmother. Now, with her grandfather's death and great uncle's incarceration, everyone expected her to step up and handle things. Only one problem with the theory, she wanted to stand up for herself first.

"It's what I have to do, CoCo."

"I understand, I really do, but maybe you should take a little time to consider your options. Maybe look into a different apartment complex, even. No one feels comfortable with you going back there since Jolie's killer is still roaming the streets."

"Did Luc put you up to talking to me?"

Guilt seeped into every inch of CoCo's expression as she reddened. "He loves you."

42

"I know. But this is something I have to do." She fisted her right hand over her cane. "I can't give up the strides I've made in my independence. I won't."

"I know, but we're concerned about your safety. There *is* a killer out there."

Felicia gave a dry laugh. "Now you sound like Mother." She shook her head. "Do you know she ranted for two whole hours about me not living alone? Like I'm twelve or something." She paused, swallowing back the grief. "I'm just not ready to think about a roommate yet."

"She's just worried. We all are, *Boo.*"

"No need to worry about me more than anyone else. I'm not a cripple anymore, in case none of you have noticed." As soon as the words were out of her mouth, Felicia could've bitten off her own tongue. "I'm sorry. I didn't mean to sound so snappy. I'm just so tired of hearing the same old arguments. My mind's made up — I'm staying on my own."

CoCo's lips pressed into a tight line.

She hadn't meant to offend CoCo, had only wanted to make it clear she could make decisions for herself. She glanced at her friend again. CoCo's knuckles were white as she gripped the steering wheel.

Felicia's jaw dropped.

"CoCo LeBlanc, is that an engagement ring on your finger?"

Jerking her left hand into her lap, CoCo nearly ditched the Jeep. She steadied the vehicle, a sheepish light glimmering in her eyes. "Uh . . . well . . ."

"My brother finally proposed again, yes?"

This time, CoCo's smile lit up the vehicle brighter than the February sun. "Yes. Three nights ago."

"Three nights! And when did you plan on telling me?"

"We wanted to tell you the next day, but that's when . . ."

The *incident.* Jolie'd been murdered.

What a way to have an engagement overshadowed.

Felicia swallowed against a dry mouth. "This is wonderful. About time. You'll be my sister for real now. When's the big date? I hope y'all aren't planning a long engagement this time."

"We were thinking of an April wedding."

"Oh, that'll be beautiful." Tears of joy sprang to Felicia's eyes. "I'm so happy for you. Took him long enough, yes?"

CoCo giggled — she actually let out a little girl titter. "I'd like an outdoor wedding in my yard. The azaleas and oleanders will be in full bloom — the magnolias too."

"It'll be beautiful, I know it will." Felicia fought not to think about the fact that her own wedding plans had been ripped apart before the bud had an opportunity to bloom.

"I'd hoped you'd be one of my bridesmaids." CoCo darted her gaze from the road to focus on Felicia's face briefly.

"Oh, I'd be honored." Felicia chewed the inside of her lip. "Let's see, April. If I work harder in therapy, I might be able to lose the cane by then."

"Don't push yourself. I just want you there."

"You know I wouldn't miss this for anything. I've prayed and prayed for this day to come."

"And our prayers have been answered."

"Yes, they certainly have."

But what about her prayers for happiness and protection for those she loved? Had she gotten a resounding "no" to those requests? First her grandfather, then her great-uncle, then Frank, and now Jolie. Would the cloud of death ever stop hovering over her head?

Afternoon sunlight bathed Lagniappe in a warm glow, despite the calendar's February date. Birds chirped, grasshoppers flicked about in the green grass. How wrong for

45

nature to celebrate new life springing up in the blooms of redbud trees while Spencer had to honor a young life ended too soon. Where were the dark clouds and rolling thunder? Irony like this made him question his calling.

He jerked his gaze across the cemetery as Felicia limped toward the assembly of chairs. Luc and CoCo flanked her. Despite their assistance, her face was pale, making her ocean-clear eyes appear even bluer. His gut clenched.

Father, I don't understand, but I accept Your will. I know Felicia does, too, but she's hurting so badly. I pray for You to surround her with the peace and comfort only You can provide.

People milled about, talking in hushed tones. Spencer noticed several members of his congregation and operators from the crisis center. People who cared about Jolie Landry. Loved her. In contrast, both Sheriff Theriot and Deputy Anderson stood under the magnolia tree in the corner of the cemetery. Their heads turned each time someone walked past, plodding to the grave-side. Their presence made pinpricks rise on the back of Spencer's neck.

Someone touched his elbow, snapping Spencer back to the task at hand.

"I got your message," Jon Garrison said.

Tall and dressed neatly in a suit, the man appeared more distinguished than he truly was.

Spencer darted his stare over the people taking seats. "Checking to see that I'm really where I said I'd be?"

"When you miss an appointment, even when you call in and notify the office, I feel compelled to follow up."

Sweat stuck Spencer's shirt to his back. "I've never lied to you about my whereabouts."

"Still gotta check things out. It's my job, you know?"

Spencer ground his teeth. He didn't need an interrogation today, of all days. He'd been reliving his past mistakes all by himself. Jon's appearance just magnified the situation.

"So, who died?"

"A young woman of my congregation. Worked for me at the crisis center, too."

"Young, huh? What happened?"

"She was murdered." Spencer couldn't help gazing at Felicia as he spoke the words.

She stared blankly at the coffin, her eyes shimmering. Luc's and CoCo's mouths moved, but Felicia gave no indication she heard anything. Truth be told, she looked like she'd fallen under some trance.

"Murdered? What's the deal?"

Spencer turned his attention back to Jon, struggling to disguise the contempt he had for the man who could pull Spencer's freedom out from under him. "Listen, I need to do *my* job now." He gave a curt nod. "If you'll excuse me."

People greeted him as he strode across the blanket of grass, but he had to touch Felicia's shoulder to get her to look him in the eye. "Are you okay?"

She nodded, her lips pressed tightly together.

Luc extended his hand. "Pastor."

Spencer shook his friend's hand but kept his stare trained on Felicia. "Felicia, will you be able to do the eulogy?" He'd advised her not to, but she'd been persistent. Determined.

"I'll be fine."

He glanced over the crowd before checking his watch. Time to start. He squeezed Felicia's shoulder in a way he hoped conveyed his reassurance, then headed back to the podium. He stared at the two policemen as they moved forward to stand at the back of the crowd. Both had their stares glued to the group of people.

Jon Garrison had moved to stand behind the crowd as well. Just what he didn't need

48

— the lawmen questioning who Jon Garrison was. And why he had attended the funeral.

With a lump the size of a *pirogue* stuck in his throat, Spencer shucked off his unease. He cleared his throat and lifted the Bible.

"This is Felicia." She adjusted the headset's microphone closer to her mouth.

"Uh, yeah. I don't know if you'll remember me. This is, uh, Winnie." The woman's voice came out squeakier than Felicia recalled.

"Hello, Winnie. Of course I remember you. I'm so glad you called me back. I've been praying for you." Felicia rose to her feet, her gaze floating over the crisis center to find Spence. He met her stare, then glanced away. She snapped her fingers and waved him to her desk.

"Yeah. Okay."

"How're you doing?"

"I'm not so mad at that hussy anymore."

"Really? That's great, Winnie." She emphasized the woman's name as Spence moved beside her. "Much healthier for you."

"Okay. If you say so. Anyways, it wasn't her fault. Not really."

Progress. At least it was a step in the right direction.

"I'm glad to hear you've let go of your anger toward the woman."

"Yeah. She may have enticed him, but he didn't have to chase after her like a dog to a bone. But that's okay. He'll get his."

"Now, Winnie, that doesn't sound good. Surely you can see that plotting revenge isn't good for you." *Lord, please let her see that revenge isn't the answer.*

The woman laughed. "Maybe not, but it sure feels good. Oh, he'll get his, all right."

"Um, I think maybe you should talk to our pastor. Remember, I told you about him?"

Spence wiped his hands on his jeans. A silly ritual that he did before he took a hard call.

"No. I don't want to talk to anybody else. Matter of fact, I don't wanna talk to you anymore, either."

The connection clicked loudly in Felicia's earpiece. Yanking the headset off, she tossed it on the desk.

"No dice, huh?" Spence's words were gentle.

"And got rather indignant when I even suggested she talk to you." Felicia shook her head. "I don't get it. She calls initially to talk to me about winning her guy back, then moves into threats of hurting the new girlfriend. Now she's not mad at the girl-friend anymore, but is plotting payback toward her ex for hurting her. Something's not right with her, Spence. She's not rational."

"But she's not threatening that woman anymore, right?"

"No, but she's bent on revenge toward her ex."

Spence straightened and ran a hand over his head. "Think she's just blowing smoke?"

She shook her head. "Something's going on with her. I feel it. She's not stable and it isn't just her pain venting."

"But she didn't act on her feelings toward the new girlfriend, and she called back. Maybe in a couple more days, she'll call again and not be so bitter toward her ex."

"I hope so." Nice thought, but she had her doubts. The woman ping-ponged with her emotions. Felicia reached for her cane.

"You know, you didn't have to come in tonight. I could've had others cover for you." He laid a hand on her shoulder. "I know how hard it's been for you."

Heat nearly seared her shoulder. She forced herself to focus despite the feelings pulling her to him. He was only her boss, yes? "I'll be okay. I need to be here. If I can help someone else, maybe I won't feel so . . ."

"So what?"

She'd almost forgotten he'd been trained to dig out secrets. "Nothing. I'm all right." Felicia got to her feet and shot him a shaky smile. "Don't worry about me."

"Have you heard anything from the sheriff?"

She let out a heavy sigh. "They haven't come up with anything yet."

He squeezed her shoulder. "They'll find who did it soon."

But as she headed to the break room, she knew nothing would be right in her world for a long time coming.

FOUR

"I still think this is a bad idea, *Boo.* No one will think less of you if you reconsider and stay home." Luc hesitated, holding the overflowing box of dishes easily on his hip.

"I said no, and meant it," Felicia replied as she tossed all the dishrags on top of the box.

"How about you at least stay until the killer is caught?"

"And if that doesn't happen anytime soon, then what? Just live at home for the rest of my life?"

"It's not a good idea for you to be living here alone after what happened."

"I'm tired of discussing it, yes?"

"When did you get so stubborn?"

"Runs in the family." She smiled to soften her words.

Luc shook his head. "Fine. But if there's even so much as a hint of violence around you, I'm going to come right back and march you straight home. I don't like you living here alone." He stormed from the apartment.

Felicia bit back her grin. He truly worried over her, and she didn't doubt he'd make good on his threat. All the more reason to see Jolie's killer brought to justice quickly. It'd ensure her independence. Or, at the very least, get Luc off her back.

She checked the cabinets a final time. All empty. Counters, too, except for a single item. The butcher block of knives. She hadn't been able to pack it. Jolie had been killed with a knife. None of their knives had been used — the sheriff had ruled out that possibility. Still, Felicia didn't know if she'd ever be able to look at a knife again and not think of Jolie's murder. She jerked the butcher block into the trash bag.

Soft footfalls sounded from the doorway. "The sheriff told me he still hasn't gotten in touch with Kipp. Would you like me to take the box of Jolie's things to my house until they do?" CoCo shoved her dark curls from her face.

Why hadn't the police located Kipp? He didn't shown up for Jolie's funeral, and no one had seen or heard from him since. Did the loan sharks get him, too? Cold fingertips trailed down Felicia's back as she started to wonder if Luc was right. She gave herself a mental shake. No, she had to stake her independence now or she'd falter.

"Fels, you okay?" CoCo touched her shoulder. Warm, caring.

"I'm fine. Um, I'll just keep her things in my closet until Kipp resurfaces." If he ever did, that is. She certainly wouldn't bring up her concerns, though. Luc would throw a fit and toss her back home in a heartbeat if he though she was scared. But Jolie's murder hadn't been random. The police agreed with her.

"Okay." CoCo pierced her with a look filled with pity.

Just what Felicia didn't want or need. She headed to her bedroom, her limp more pronounced from spending the whole day packing up the apartment. It was her day off from physical therapy, but she'd overworked her muscles just as if she'd done four sets.

Alyssa LeBlanc, CoCo's sister visiting from New Orleans, breezed down the hallway. "All your address-change requests have been delivered to the post office, madam."

"*Merci*. I appreciate it."

While the others toted boxes across the complex, Felicia finished packing her bedroom. Her hands paused as she reached for

55

her jewelry box. She opened the lid, the hinge creaking. The single solitaire blinked up at her, the overhead light causing the diamond to sparkle as if the promise hadn't been broken. Felicia blinked back tears and regret — and anger. Anger that Frank had died at their engagement party.

"Almost done in here?" Luc hovered in the doorway.

Her brother couldn't see her crying — it'd just confirm his belief that she shouldn't be alone. "Only this last one."

He lifted the cardboard box with ease and hollered over his shoulder. "Tara says to tell you she's almost done with setting up your kitchen."

Felicia couldn't stop the edges of her mouth from tweaking into a smile as she moved to the hallway. CoCo's youngest sister was a fireball. Tara had more spunk than either CoCo or Alyssa. No one would tell Tara LeBlanc what she could or couldn't do. They wouldn't dare. Maybe Felicia should take a lesson or two from her.

Spence met her in the hall. "That about everything?" His eyes sparkled, almost brighter than her ring.

Felicia's heartbeat quickened, and she struggled to ignore it. No, she couldn't be attracted to him. He was her boss. Besides, it was too soon, a little over a year since Frank had died. She hadn't stopped grieving. Had she? No, she only felt like this because Spence was one of the few people who didn't stare at her with pity. He admired her strength — hadn't he told her several times since her surgery? It was not attraction she felt, but gratitude, yes? Had to be. "Yeah. I just need to turn these keys in to Mr. McRae."

"Let me. You need to see what they're doing in your apartment. Make sure they put everything where you can find it." He took the two keys from her hand and grinned. Did his smile have to be as bright as his eyes?

Her fingers tingled where they'd made contact with his. Not attraction, gratitude, she reminded herself. She'd do well to distinguish between the two.

She double-checked the entry closet. A single sweater hung on a hanger. Felicia snatched the bright yellow pullover free, clutching it against her chest. The distinct perfume Jolie always wore lingered on the soft knit. Felicia shook her head. Jolie had borrowed the sweater the night she'd been murdered. Why was it hanging alone in the closet? She'd boxed up everything earlier, hadn't she? Strange, very strange.

A boisterous laugh rang out from the complex. Felicia turned, catching sight of CoCo and Alyssa good-naturedly nudging each other as they carried empty boxes to the Dumpster, apologizing to a young woman they nearly jostled off the walkway. A lump the size of Louisiana lodged in her throat as memories accosted her. Jolie bouncing on Felicia's bed to share details of a great date. Teasing her about not leaving wet towels on the floor. Sharing Scriptures and secrets together in stolen moments.

She allowed a final few tears to trail down her cheeks before leaving the apartment and shutting the door behind her. Shutting off the pain, she closed off another death of someone she loved.

The afternoon breeze carried a hint of rain. Felicia trudged across the courtyard, leaning heavily on her cane and clutching her sweater. This was it. Everything had been transferred to the new apartment. She took a moment to look back at her old one.

I won't forget you, Jolie. I'll find your killer and then you can rest in peace. I owe you that much.

Did she have to look so fragile? Broken, yet strong?

Spencer hauled in a deep breath and

turned from the window. Felicia's family and friends were putting the finishing touches on setting up the new apartment. How they'd managed to get everything moved and unboxed, much less put away, in just a day was beyond him. The love these people had for Felicia warmed his heart. But he still couldn't help wishing she'd stayed at her family's home instead of moving back into these apartments. Wouldn't painful memories stalk her every step here? Was she even safe?

He drew himself up short. It wasn't any of his business. She was a nice girl, a good employee, a strong Christian. He had no right to worry about her emotional state. He'd best get those random thoughts right out of his head.

"So, how's it look? Anything we need to change?" CoCo asked Felicia as soon as she entered.

"Wow. I had no idea y'all would get everything put up for me."

Tara snorted. "Well, if you can't find a certain pot or pan, don't say I didn't warn ya."

"I appreciate what you've done." Felicia glanced over each person in turn. "All of you."

"*Allons,* let's look at your bedroom."

CoCo wrapped an arm around Felicia and led her down the hall.

No need for him to stay any longer. He stepped into their path. "I need to get back to the center."

Felicia nodded. "I'll see you on my shift."

"You don't have to come in tonight. I imagine you're beat."

"No. I'll be there." Determination rested in her delicate features.

He could tell it wouldn't do him any good to argue with her. "See you later, then."

He headed to the front door, wiping his hands against the rough denim of his jeans. To his surprise, Luc met him on the sidewalk. "Mind if I walk you out?"

By the look in Luc's eyes, he had something serious on his mind. "Sure."

They reached his truck before Luc spoke. "I'm concerned about Felicia."

"I am, too." Spencer dug the keys from his pocket, jangling them at the door.

"I wonder if I could ask you to keep an eye on her while she's at the center? At first I didn't want her to work, but at least if she's there with you, she's safer than being here alone."

"I'll do what I can, Luc."

"*Merci.* I appreciate it." He popped his knuckles. "She has a stubborn streak a mile

60

wide, but if she comes into any danger, I've already told her I'll pack her up and take her back home."

Spencer would almost pay to see that. He could imagine the fire in Felicia's eyes if Luc even tried it. He suddenly got a vision of her eyes dancing with anger. Interesting that he imagined she'd be all the more attractive. No, he had to keep his mind free of such thoughts. "I'll keep an eye on her as best I can."

Luc nodded and retreated to the sidewalk as Spencer backed out of the parking place and steered toward the center. Conflicting thoughts battled for his attention. On one hand, Spencer could understand Luc's protectiveness toward Felicia — she was his little sister, had been handicapped until recently and had suffered such grief in the past year. On the flip side, he could relate to Felicia's attitude — needing her independence, wanting to deal with the pain herself and not wanting people to walk on eggshells around her. The situation called for a very delicate balance, and Spencer felt as if he'd landed in the middle of the crossfire.

He parked his truck in his designated spot and marched into the center. Ringing phones and voices merged into a steady hum.

Good to be back on familiar ground.

Once in his office, he read his messages from his assistant. A cold sweat broke out on his forehead as his heartbeat raced. Sheriff Theriot had called and needed to speak to him ASAP.

Had they run a background check on him? He gripped the paper tighter. Garrison. Spencer knew there'd be trouble for him when Jon Garrison had showed up at Jolie's funeral. The sheriff probably couldn't wait to ask Garrison why he'd been there. Jon Garrison would dump the whole sorry story out to the police. Just what Spencer didn't need.

What to do? The church's elders knew about his past, but they were the only ones he'd told. He'd never lied, he just hadn't expounded on his experiences. But he couldn't sweep his past under the rug with the police. His congregation and friends, yes, but not law enforcement. They knew everything. Or would soon enough.

If he ignored the message, they'd either call again or just show up. No, better to just get it over with over the phone. He dialed the number on the message and asked to speak to the sheriff.

"Sheriff Theriot."

"This is Spencer Bertrand returning your

call." His tongue thickened instantly.

"Pastor. I'm looking over your statement about Jolie Landry."

"Yes?" *Lord, please give me strength.*

"I was wondering if you kept records, logs or something, of all the calls that come into the center."

"We keep logs, and I mean that in the loosest sense of the word. Each operator keeps a record of their calls, a brief description of the situation, what they advised, if it was transferred to me, that kind of thing."

"We'll need to see copies of Jolie Landry's records for the past month."

His heart raced. There couldn't be a tie between Jolie's death and the center. His center. His personal atonement. "Sheriff, I want to help, I truly do, but those records are confidential. I'm sure you understand."

"I figured you'd say that, but had to ask. We'll be getting a warrant to get copies of them, Pastor."

His tongue felt twenty sizes too big for his mouth. "We'll abide by any warrant."

"I know you will."

Spencer hung up the phone. His shirt stuck to his back, glued with sweat. Relief that his secret was still safe washed over him, but for how long? This was it — his worst nightmare come true. How long would it take the sheriff to check on him? Being a preacher didn't exempt him from police inquiries.

He lowered his head into his hands. When the sheriff got around to it, Spencer would be their number-one suspect. Case closed. He could hear the prison bars locking into place behind him.

Father, help me.

FIVE

"I'm looking for Sadie Thompson." Felicia made certain her voice didn't quiver as she held on to the phone.

"She's not here right now. Who is this?" the nasal-toned voice pressed her.

"I'll call back later." Felicia hung up the phone with a clank, her hands trembling. The police didn't seem to have any clues about Jolie's case yet, so she had decided to give them a helping hand.

She glanced around the kitchen with its sunny marigold curtains. She couldn't believe she was taking an active role in this investigation. But Jolie'd been her best friend. Felicia owed it to her to see her killer brought to justice.

Bam! Bam! Bam!

Felicia jumped, and her overworked leg muscles spasmed along with her heart. *Get a grip, girl, it's just someone knocking on the door.* No murderers waiting to pounce on her. She grabbed her cane and hobbled to the door. "Who is it?"

"It's me, Wes."

She flipped the dead bolt, glancing at her watch as she did. Only an hour before the driver would arrive to take her to work. "Wes, come on in."

The handsome man followed her inside, but didn't look as dashing as usual. His hair had a greasy sheen to it, dark circles weighted his eyes and no air of pricey cologne wafted in his wake. Grief. Felicia knew the signs all too well. "Sit down."

He flopped onto the couch, grabbing the throw pillow, splaying his fingers across the green chenille tassels. "I don't know what to do."

She sat in the chair adjacent to the couch and finger-brushed her shower-damp hair. "I miss her, too."

"I don't know if I can go on without her. I loved her. I hadn't told her yet, had meant to the night she . . . she . . ." His eyes filled with tears.

Mirroring tears burned her eyes. "I need to ask you something. Why were you spending time with Sadie?"

"It was only once. She'd asked me to meet her about some religious issues. Whoever saw us and told Jolie, well, they were trying to stir up trouble between us."

Deep inside, Felicia had known he hadn't cheated on Jolie. "I'm sorry."

He blinked several times, his fingers toying with the tassel. "It's not just that. The police are giving me a hard time."

"How so?"

"They're treating me like a suspect."

"They're questioning all of us, Wes, not just you. Everybody who had contact with Jolie over the past couple of weeks." She laid a hand over his. "They're trying to find any hint of who could've done such a horrible thing."

"No, the sheriff's asked to search my house and car."

"Whatever for?"

"I think he's looking to pin this on me."

"He can't suspect you." The implications rammed against her common sense. "Why, that's ludicrous. You were in love with her."

"You know the old story — they always look to the husband or boyfriend first." He let out a deep sigh. "I have to give him an answer today. If I refuse, he says he'll get a warrant."

What could Sheriff Theriot be thinking? Then Felicia remembered how she'd recently watched the national news run an in-depth special on overeager law officers and their twisting of evidence to gain convictions. But here in Lagniappe? Surely the sheriff would do a thorough investigation — he'd always impressed her with his values. He was a Christian man, a pillar in the church and the community. Caring and kind.

She squeezed his hands. "I want you to listen to me carefully. You need to hire yourself a lawyer."

"A lawyer?" His voice hitched.

"Yes, a lawyer. Try calling Dwayne Williams. My brother's fiancée used him last year and was pleased with how he handled her case."

His eyes took on an earnest look. "Felicia, I promise you, I didn't kill Jolie."

As she studied him, she knew he told the truth. "I know you didn't."

"Who do you think did?"

Wasn't that the million-dollar question?

"I think it's someone Kipp was involved with. All those gambling debts, loan sharks, threats . . . I think someone killed Jolie to scare Kipp."

He nodded. "Me, too. She said Kipp had gotten in with some nasty characters."

"She told me the same thing. I told the sheriff that."

"So did I, but I don't think he believes a

word I say."

"It may seem that way, but the truth will eventually come out."

"I hope so. You know, there are a lot of people on death row who claim they're innocent." He shook his head and dropped his gaze to the floor. "I don't want to end up one of them."

She didn't want him to, either. If Luc and CoCo had not figured out that Uncle Justin killed Grandfather, either of them could very well have been among those innocents in prison. What had happened to the justice system? In the past several years, it seemed that the truth no longer mattered — only that someone paid for a crime. Lady Justice was supposed to be blind, but that didn't mean the police were supposed to be, as well.

"I don't think the police are following up on Kipp's associates." His words were mumbled.

"They haven't been able to locate him yet. We'll just keep praying they do, and that he can give them names." But that posed an interesting question — why hadn't the police found him? Sure, they said they'd been looking, but how hard could it be to find someone in an area as small as the Lagniappe community?

He got to his feet. "Thanks, Felicia. I think I'll call that Dwayne Williams."

"Good idea." She walked him to the door. "Try to think positive, although I know it's hard." She opened the door and then drew back when she saw a shadow hovered on the threshold. She gasped, then exhaled slowly as her eyes adjusted to the approaching dusk.

Luc filled the doorway, his brows scrunched into a straight line and his eyes narrowed. He shot a glare at her visitor as he made his exit.

Wes nodded and edged by her brother. "Luc."

"Wesley."

"You could've just sent the driver, yes?" Felicia waved Luc inside. My, wasn't this the day for visitors?

"What was he doing here?" Luc shut the door firmly.

"Visiting. A common social occurrence, from what I gather."

"He's a suspect in Jolie's murder."

Her sauciness raised a level. She faced off with her brother, her hand planted firmly on her hip. "Just like you were in Grandfather's murder."

"But I was innocent."

"So is Wes."

70

"How do you know?"

"Same way I knew with you. He's not capable of killing someone he loved."

"You can't be sure of that."

"Yes, I can." She sank back onto the chair. "Are you questioning my ability to judge a person's character?"

Luc dropped to the couch and ran a hand over his head. "Yes . . . no . . . I don't know, *Boo*. All I know is someone killed Jolie in your apartment, and you're all alone. I don't like it."

Just when she'd worked up a good bit of righteous anger, he had to throw in brotherly concern. Her frustration abated, she softened her tone. "I know you are worried, and I love you all the more for it. But, Luc, I'm going to be fine."

"There're no guarantees in life."

"I know that better than anyone. But I also know God won't leave me alone. And He loves me more than you ever can."

He opened his mouth, then snapped it shut. "Okay, you win. But I'm not going to stop worrying about you." He smiled, but it didn't reach his eyes. "Mom's taking your leaving again pretty hard."

"I'm sure. She called me four times last night with her continuous theatrics."

Luc shook his head. "It's more than that.

She's been nipping the brandy again."

"And I suppose that's my fault, yes?" Felicia let out a loud sigh. It was always something with Hattie Trahan, drama queen extraordinaire.

"I'm not blaming you, I'm just telling you what's what."

She gritted her teeth. She would not gather her things for a guilt trip. Her mother used drinking to manipulate people, Felicia and Luc along with everyone else. "Wouldn't be the first time."

"True. But it's a depressed drinking now."

"Then make her go to counseling, rehab, whatever."

Luc snorted. "Like I can make her do anything?"

"Well, you aren't making me move back home, if that's what you were hoping to accomplish."

"I'm just trying to keep you safe."

"And I'm just telling you I don't need you to be my protector. I'm fine." She stood. "I'll be okay, Luc, but I'm worn out from these constant arguments. If you can't stop bringing it up, I'll hire my own driver — one you're not paying for."

He stood as well and slung an arm around her shoulders, pulling her gently against him. "I'm sorry, *Boo.* I don't mean to nag.

I'll work on it, okay?"

She nodded. He'd work on the nagging, but he wouldn't change his mind. And now, after talking with Wes, she was even more determined to find Jolie's murderer. Fast.

Spencer spent the day reviewing Jolie's call records. Not a single violent one in the past three months. He should've been relieved, but he knew the sheriff would still eventually pull a background check on him. No way around it. Maybe he should just talk to Theriot when he served his warrant — lay out all his cards. But was that really such a hot idea? The sheriff hadn't been in the most responsive frame of mind since Spencer made him get a warrant. Still, what else could he do?

The church elders had been understanding at the time of his hiring, had promised they'd allow him to tell his parishioners himself in due time. What would his congregation think? Would they demand the pastoral committee members reconsider their decision? It'd happened at his first church appointment. The sting of rejection and condemnation still bit against his memory.

Speaking of not putting things off, he needed to reschedule his appointment with

Jon Garrison. Didn't that thought just fill him with joy and rapture? Small courthouse office, the stench of disinfectant used to cover the smell of urine and sour whiskey and the elevator always reeking of body odor. Who wouldn't want to visit? Only one more year, and he wouldn't have to make these monthly appointments. Unless Sheriff Theriot caused him grief.

Michael stuck his head into the office. "Pastor, there's a woman calling on my line. She's asking for Jolie and refuses to talk to anyone else."

Wiping his hands against his jeans, Spencer stood and strode to the door. "What'd you tell her?"

"Just that Jolie isn't on the schedule for tonight." Spencer's assistant shrugged. "That's true."

"Right." Spencer made quick strides to Michael's desk, set off from the row of operators. He reached for the phone, wiping his hands on his jeans again. "This is Pastor Bertrand. May I help you?"

"I want to talk to Jolie." The woman's voice cracked.

Near hysteria.

Spencer dropped into Michael's chair. "I'm sorry, Jolie isn't working tonight, but I'd love to help you."

"But I need to talk to Jolie. I need to warn her."

Adrenaline spiked his heartbeat. "Warn her about what?"

"I shouldn't even be talking to you. I need to talk to Jolie."

Calm. Steady. One wrong word and she'd hang up. Spencer couldn't lose her now — this could be the clue needed in the murder investigation. "Jolie's a wonderful young lady, but she's not here. I can try to help you. What do you want to warn her about?"

Silence filled the connection. Not even the sound of the woman's breathing could be heard.

Spencer took calming breaths. *Please, don't have hung up.* "Hello?"

"I shouldn't have called."

The click vibrated against his ear, and he let the receiver fall back to its cradle. Lifting his gaze to meet Michael's, he sighed. "I need to phone Sheriff Theriot."

Six

"Vermilion Parish Christian Counseling Hotline, this is Felicia."

"Uh, this is, um, Winnie."

Felicia stood and stared over the cubicle wall, searching for Spence. No sign of him. "Hi, Winnie. I'm glad you called back. How're you doing?" She waved at Sally, the operator next to her, and gestured toward Spence's door.

"Better."

Sally rushed toward the office. Felicia dropped back to her chair. "That's wonderful. You're still not having feelings of anger or bitterness toward your ex's new girlfriend, yes?"

"Nope, she basically left him."

Where was Spence?

"But he hasn't come running back to me like I thought he would."

Finally, Spence emerged and made his way toward Felicia's station. Sheriff Theriot

76

dogged him. "Had he given you any indication that he would?" What was the sheriff doing behind closed doors with Spence?

Winnie's laugh was dry. "He should've."

Felicia pointed at the name she'd logged, then plugged in the set of training earphones and handed them to Spence. He needed to hear this conversation. The sheriff hovered behind them. "So, are you and he speaking?"

"I tried. I went by to try to comfort him after she was gone, but he totally blew me off." A hint of anger crept into her tone.

"Maybe he's just as hurt over her leaving as you were over him leaving you."

Winnie grunted. "I hope so. I hope the pain is ripping him up inside."

"You don't mean that."

"I do. And I'm going to make sure he hurts more. Nobody dumps me like he did."

"I know you're hurting, Winnie, but revenge isn't the way to go."

"Why not? Because the Bible says so?" She laughed with a high-pitched lilt. "I play by my own rules, and that's served me just fine all my life."

"But the anger and bitterness only eat you up, Winnie. It hurts you more than your ex or his new girlfriend."

Winnie laughed again. "I doubt that."

"You must have a reason for calling me. I think you want someone to listen and care about you. I do, Winnie."

"You don't even know me."

"So why call me?" Felicia held her breath. These calls always came down to the basic question — was someone crying out for help, or did they want to brag? Winnie hadn't exactly fallen into either category.

"I don't know why, really. The first time I called, I was actually looking for someone else."

"Who?" Had Winnie made a connection with another operator? Maybe given them a different name?

"That's not important anymore. You were nice, so I thought we could be friends."

There was that hot-and-cold mood swing again. "I'd like to be your friend, Winnie."

"Not anymore. He changed me. Made me act in ways I never dreamed I would. But he'll be hurting a lot more than me before I get through with him. When I'm done, he'll wish he was dead."

A knot tied in Felicia's gut. "What are you planning?" Her gaze locked with Spence's.

More laughter. "Guess that's for me to know and you not to find out."

"Win—"

Too late. The call disconnected.

"What do you think?" Felicia unplugged her phone from the system operating board.

Spence laid the headphones on the desk. His face wrinkled into a tight mask of worry. He let out a deep breath, as if he'd been holding it for years, and tilted his head toward the sheriff.

Felicia pushed to her feet. "Spence, may I see you in your office, please?" She glanced at Sheriff Theriot, then back to Spence. "Please."

He led the way to his office. She pushed the door closed behind them and stood before his desk as he took a seat. "You're not thinking of telling the sheriff about Winnie, are you?"

"It might be a good idea, considering all that's happened."

Strange — Spence normally tried everything humanly possible to keep the center's business private. Even when he had to push a battered woman to go to a shelter, if she gave her name, Spence wouldn't call the police. Yet over Winnie he would? Sure, she was a ticking time bomb, but what could they tell the police? A scorned woman had threatened revenge against her ex? That went back to Old Testament times.

"But why now? We've never filed reports with the police before."

He scrubbed his face absentmindedly. "I took a call earlier. Lady wanted to speak to Jolie."

She swallowed, the lump sitting sideways in her throat not budging.

"She wanted to warn Jolie."

Her heart stuttered. "Warn her about what?"

"I don't know. She hung up on me. I called the sheriff." He leaned back in his chair, balancing on the back two legs. "I can't take a chance that someone else associated with the center could be hurt."

"That's silly. There's no correlation."

"There isn't?" He dropped the front two chair legs to the floor. A thud echoed off the walls covered with thank-you cards from callers helped over the past two years. "You know this how?"

"I believe the people Kipp owed money to are the ones responsible for Jolie's death."

"The sheriff's getting a warrant for Jolie's logs from here. We need to make sure there isn't an association."

She couldn't believe a link existed, because if one did, Luc had been right and she wasn't safe. The lump in her throat dropped to rest in the pit of her stomach. "You really believe the center's involved?"

"More than you can ever know, I don't

want there to be a correlation." His eyes dimmed, and he dropped his gaze to the desk.

This had to be eating him up inside. Felicia knew how dedicated Spence was to the center. He'd only bring in the police if he felt that was the only option left. She laid a hand on his shoulder. "I'm sorry."

He popped up his head and met her gaze. His piercing eyes, combined with the tingling traveling up her arm from the touch, made her dizzy. She jerked her hand back to her side. "I mean, I know how much you like to keep the center's business private."

Spence hauled himself to his feet. "Trust me, if there were any other way, I'd take it. I don't have a choice this time." He nodded toward the office window. "Guess we'd better not keep the sheriff waiting much longer."

She glanced over her shoulder. Sheriff Theriot leaned against the wall, appearing nonchalant, but his steady stare never left her and Spence. She swallowed hard. "Okay. I'll bring him up to speed on Winnie's calls."

"Merci." He touched her arm, and his gaze softened.

Her mouth went dry. This man, her *boss,* couldn't affect her this way. She gave him a slight smile before turning and opening the office door.

Better to face an inquiring sheriff than deal with her own confusing emotions.

Look in the dictionary under *southern belle* and Felicia Trahan's picture would be beside it, Spence thought as he watched her talk to Sheriff Theriot. She brought the definition of a refined lady to life. Strong as a lightning rod, yet as gentle as Spanish moss fluttering from a cypress tree. Answering the sheriff's questions with precision, adding no elaborations, she kept her emotions from slipping into her voice. Spencer couldn't help but be impressed. After all she'd been through, Felicia still came across as smooth as the bayou in the morning.

He snatched back his thoughts. He could never act on his feelings. Felicia Trahan was off limits and always would be. He'd never be worthy of her.

Lord, could You give me some guidance on this? I know I shouldn't be feeling the way I am around her, but these feelings keep popping up. I could use some wisdom on the situation.

"You have anything else to add, Pastor?"

The sheriff interrupted Spencer's prayer, pulling him back into the conversation. "No.

Nothing else."

The sheriff pocketed his notebook and stood. "I'll make this report and see what I can find out. Until we get some answers, I'd encourage you to think about closing down the center."

"What?" Felicia cried.

Little bursts of panic blasted against Spencer's heart. "I don't think we need to go that far, Sheriff."

"I'm just saying . . . the murder, these calls, the woman who wanted to warn Jolie . . . it all sounds connected to me."

No, he couldn't close the center. Wouldn't. Spencer stiffened his spine and squared off with the sheriff. "Until such a link is affirmed, the center will stay open." Was that a sigh of relief from Felicia?

The sheriff shrugged and opened the office door. "Your call, Pastor. For now. If we find proof the center's somehow related with Jolie's murder, then I'll have no other option but to close it down. Officially."

"Sheriff," Felicia interrupted, "is there anything new on Jolie's case?"

"I'm not at liberty to discuss the case with you, Felicia." He softened his expression. "Just leave this to the police and try to get on with your life."

As soon as the sheriff turned the corner,

Spencer dropped into his chair.

"They haven't the first lead, I'll bet. You won't let them close the center, will you?" Felicia's eyes glistened.

"I'll do my best not to."

Michael stuck his head into the office. "Boss, we're heading out. And, Felicia, your brother's on line one. Sounds important."

Without asking permission, she yanked up Spencer's phone. "Luc? What's wrong?" She nibbled her bottom lip and wound the phone cord around her finger. "Oh. That's okay. I can just call a cab." She let out a grunt that sounded suspiciously like a growl. "I can arrange for my own ride home, Luc. I'm neither a child nor an invalid."

Uh-oh. That sauciness bubbled into her voice. Spencer chanced a glimpse at her face. He'd been right — she was really attractive when her eyes sparkled with anger. He knocked on the desk. "I can take you home if you need a ride." Where'd that come from?

She smiled. "Never mind. Spence volunteered to give me a lift home." She unwound the cord from her finger. "Okay. Love you, too."

"Driver problems?"

She replaced the phone in its cradle. "Apparently the driver's come down with a bug of some sort, and Luc's driving CoCo, Tara and Mrs. LeBlanc to N'Awlins."

"What're they doing in New Orleans?"

"Going to visit Alyssa and Jackson. Seems the lovebirds are eloping." She swallowed back her personal regret. "It's been a year. I guess that's a long-enough engagement. Still, I'd have thought Alyssa would want a big wedding."

"You never know."

"I guess you know CoCo and Luc have set a wedding date, yes?"

"They've asked me to officiate."

"That'll be nice. I appreciate you giving me a ride home."

"No problem." He glanced at the clock and grabbed his keys. "It's quitting time, anyway. How about a cup of coffee before I drop you off?"

"Oh." Her eyes widened. "Uh, yeah. That sounds nice."

He picked up on the hesitation in her voice. "Unless you have other plans."

"No." Splotches of pink tiptoed across her cheeks. She paused a moment before gifting him with a bright smile. "Thank you. I'd like that."

Funny how her blushing did strange things to his gut.

The center sat in an eerie silence as they crossed the floor to the exit. He cut the lights, locked the doors and led her to the parking lot. She slipped into his truck as if she belonged there.

Stop thinking such things. Could never happen.

The tiny diner down the road had a neon Open sign blinking in its window along with the green Mardi Gras decoration. He steered the car into the lot. "This okay?"

"Fine."

Nary a person sat in the diner, save the waitress and a short-order cook, grumbling in the back. The air reeked of old grease and fried okra. After selecting a booth near the front door, having their coffee cups filled and Spencer ordering a piece of pecan pie, they were left alone. "You know, what you said to Winnie was good."

"What?" Felicia set her cup onto the table.

"About the bitterness eating her up, not her ex."

"It's true."

"Personal experience talking?"

She tugged her hand into her lap so quickly, the cup rattled against the chipped table. "What do you mean?"

"Letting go of bitterness. Losing your fiancé."

"Oh." Her gaze trailed her hand into her lap.

Not a good sign. He lowered his voice. "Felicia, have you let go of your anger about losing Frank?"

She lifted her head. "I didn't lose him. He was murdered. Shot. His life taken by the hand of another person." Tears pooled in those hypnotically blue eyes of hers. "It's hard to forgive a criminal, you know? Someone who cared so little about another human's life."

The waitress plopped his pecan pie down in front of him. "Anything else?"

He shook his head, swallowing against the tight lump in his throat. "We're fine."

The waitress slipped the ticket under the edge of the plate and sashayed back to her post at the counter. The napkin holder scraped across the cracked Formica as she pulled it to her for refilling.

Spencer whispered a prayer, took a bite and studied Felicia. "Sounds to me like you're more angry than grieving."

"Maybe I am. Frank's killer stole my future. My life."

"It's been over a year, Felicia. If you've worked through the grief, don't you think it's time you worked through your anger and toward forgiveness?"

"I don't know if I can forgive Frank's murderer." She gave a shrug. "I don't know if I ever can."

His chest tightened with her words. "But you realize that's not healthy, right?"

Her eyes blinked brighter, and her hand trembled slightly as she took another sip from her cup. "Do you think the sheriff will shut down the center?"

Whoa, she shifted gears fast. He swallowed a bite of pie, the sugary texture going down slowly. "I don't think they'll be able to do that. At least, not now."

Father, please don't let them shut me down. This center is my penance.

"I hope not. I don't know what I'd do."

"Let's not worry about it unless it happens, okay?" He laid his hand over hers. The warmth spread deep within his spirit. Setting his fork against the remaining pie, Spencer nodded at her cup. "Want a refill?"

"Uh, no." She eased her hand out from under his.

He tossed a couple of bills on the table and led her to the door. Keeping his hand under her elbow as he assisted her to the truck gave him a feeling of peace. Completeness. Happiness.

She faced him as he climbed into his seat and started the engine. "I know I need to forgive, Spence. I'm praying hard about it."

"I understand how you're feeling now. But I'll be praying for you to find real forgiveness."

She gripped her cane, tapping her nail against the handle. "I just don't understand violent people. They make me ill."

Her words turned his stomach to stone. He whipped into the vacant space at her apartment parking lot. "Everyone makes mistakes, Felicia. Especially those in prison. Don't they deserve forgiveness?"

She opened the door and used her cane to step from the vehicle. "They do. I'm just not sure I'm a big-enough person to give it."

Spencer's heart ached as she walked away. She'd confirmed his fears. She'd never be able to forgive him if she knew the truth.

He was as bad as those men behind bars. Worse. At least they didn't hide what they were. He'd been there, paid his dues, served his time and now walked among the good citizens of Lagniappe.

And none of them knew his secret.

SEVEN

Spencer Bertrand perplexed the tar out of her. Sometimes she forgot he was a preacher and a counselor, and then he'd point out the Christian stance on issues. Like the whole forgiveness thing — something she wasn't quite ready to address. In principal, she knew she should forgive and move on with her life. The actual application was a totally different story.

Felicia finished her last set of leg presses with a vengeance born of frustration.

"Hey, sweet thang, the weights aren't your enemy."

Concentration broken, she stared at Mark. "I'm sorry." She eased off the weight bench, grabbing a towel to pass over her face. "My mind was a million miles away."

"And focusing on something mighty fierce, I might add."

"Pardon." She reached for her cane.

"No need to apologize. Use whatever you

90

can to get through your sets. Physical therapy's grueling work, I know, but you did great today."

"*Merci.* I'm gonna hit the showers."

"Your car pulled up a few seconds ago."

"I'll make it quick." She gave him a sincere smile. "See ya tomorrow."

The shower soothed her quivering muscles, but did nothing to wash out the cobwebs of confusion clouding her mind. She gave the driver the address she wanted to visit, her mind swirling with possibilities. She'd replayed her conversation with Spence over too many times to count. Could his sudden distance of the past few days have been because of her attitude toward Frank's murderer? Did he think her callous for her struggles with forgiveness?

Maybe he was right. Maybe it was time to really let go of the past and move forward with her life. She'd grown weary of being the poor victim. First cerebral palsy, then Frank's murder. Wasn't it past time to get over the bitterness and lead the life God intended her to have?

"Ms. Felicia?"

She focused on her driver at the open door. "Yes?"

"We're here, ma'am. Are you sure you gave me the correct address?"

Felicia stared at the shotgun houses along the north side of the bayou. Boards were missing, glass broken from the windows, doors didn't close properly. She swallowed. How could people live like this?

"Ms. Felicia?"

"Oh. Sorry. Yes, this is the correct place." She stepped from the car, ignoring the chill settling into her joints. Setting her chin, she smiled at the driver. "I'll only be a few minutes."

He nodded, but she could almost see him dialing Luc as soon as she walked away.

"Don't call my brother, please."

"Yes, ma'am."

She made her way up the cracked walkway. Kipp Landry really lived here? For a moment, Felicia wondered if maybe Jolie had the wrong number in her address book. Then she glanced up and down the street. Didn't matter if the number was right or wrong — all the houses along the street were in the same deplorable condition.

Mustering all the resolve she had, Felicia climbed the stairs to the front porch. The wood creaked and popped. She hesitated only a moment before rapping on the door with the end of her cane.

Creaks came from the other side of the door just before it swung open. A young man with greasy hair hanging into his half-hooded eyes glared at her. "Yeah?"

She wet her lips. "I'm looking for Kipp Landry."

"You and everybody else, lady."

"He's not here?"

"Like I told the police, ain't seen him in about a week." He shook the hair from his eyes. "You with the police?"

"N-no. I'm just a friend, looking for him."

"Hey, I'll be your friend." His wide leer turned her stomach.

"If you see Kipp, tell him Felicia came by to see him, okay?"

"Yeah. Sure." He slammed the door in her face.

So much for being her friend.

Her driver opened the door without question. She slipped inside and gave him another address.

"Are you sure, ma'am?"

Why did everyone always second-guess her? Annoyance built in her chest. "Yes, I'm sure." She didn't like how clipped her tone came out, but she was quite sick of everyone's attitude toward her decisions.

The car bumped along the bayou roads. Except for the few choice apartments, most of the residences clustered outside the city limits of Lagniappe. Still, it didn't take long to reach the jazz club. She jerked open the door before the driver could. No sense warning him not to call Luc about this stop. Her brother played his saxophone regularly here. Someone would surely mention her appearance to Luc later.

The haze of smoke hung just below eye level. Felicia bit back the cough clogging her throat at the smell. She'd better breathe through her mouth. Trying that, she almost gagged. How could the people squeezed into such a small space stand it?

She wove around the tables to reach the bar. The bartender shot her a funny look. "What can I get you?"

"Oh. Nothing. I'm looking for someone."

"Most people are, darlin'." He chuckled, then arched a brow. "Hey, aren't you Luc Trahan's sister?"

Couldn't hide in a town this small. "Yes." She leaned over the counter to be heard over the zydeco band on the stage. "I'm looking for Sadie Thompson. You seen her?"

"Not in a while." He paused. "Whatcha lookin' for Sadie for?"

"I just wanted to ask her something." Like why she'd visited Jolie hours before her murder.

"Mmm-hmm. Well, she hasn't been in the past few nights."

Felicia glanced over the people crowded around the small round tables. She didn't spot the woman's bottle-blond hair. "Thanks," she mumbled to the bartender before heading to the door.

She slipped into the car and instructed the driver to take her home. Sherlock Holmes she wasn't. Total strikeout. Oh-for-two. She'd need some answers pretty quickly. Once Luc found out she'd visited the "bad" parts of town, he'd blow up like a puffer fish and would do his best to limit her field trips in the future. She stared out the window.

Funny how she'd never realized just how far away the projects were from her world. The car came to a stop in the parking lot of her apartment building. She accepted her driver's assistance from the car. "I'll see you tomorrow."

"Yes, ma'am." As was his routine, he waited until she rounded the corner to her complex before the echo of the door slamming followed her inside the apartment.

She locked the door, set her purse on the table in the foyer and turned.

And stared with a gaping mouth.

Her beautifully arranged living room was wrecked. Pillows all over the floor. Books tossed from the shelves. Drawers dumped onto the floor.

She gripped her cane tighter. Had the door been locked? She'd been so pre-occupied that she couldn't remember. She retrieved her cell phone from her purse to call the sheriff, but when footsteps thudded down the hallway, she froze in place.

Kipp Landry stumbled into the room, jerking to a stop when he saw her. "Felicia."

Her heart caught. She pressed the first speed-dial number on her cell phone, the one for the center, and held it down while slipping the phone into her pocket. Why hadn't she set a speed dial for the police? "Kipp, what're you doing here?" She glanced around the mess in the living room. "What've you done?"

He took a step toward her. His hair looked as if it hadn't seen a brush in days, his clothes were rumpled and stained and the stench of a homeless person clung to him. "Heard you were looking for me."

Well, well, well . . . the greasy kid did know how to get in touch with Kipp. Or had Kipp been hiding there, after all? "So you broke into my apartment?" She eased around the couch.

"I need money. They'll kill me if I don't pay them. Just like they killed Jolie."

"Who are they?"

"The loan sharks. They're watching me like a hawk, waiting to see if I turn on them. If I do, I'm a dead man." His body shook. "I can't tell you who they are."

Was he on drugs? With the wild edge in his eyes, he sure looked dangerous. She prayed whoever answered at the center would listen and not hang up. "But you can steal from me, yes?" Anger pushed against her heart. "What kind of man are you, Kipp Landry?"

"One who's running out of time." His hand locked around her wrist. "Are you gonna give me the money or not?"

She jerked her arm free. "No. The police are after you, Kipp. You have to turn yourself in."

All the rage left his face. "You think I killed my sister?"

Up until this afternoon, she'd have said no, but now . . . seeing him like this, like a junkie looking for his next fix? She tightened her grip on the cell phone in her pocket, praying someone could hear the conversation. Kipp's yelling had to tip somebody off that he wasn't sane. She had to keep him talking. "Hiding from the police makes you look guilty."

His face contorted into a grimace. "I didn't kill Jolie. I loved her." His voice came out as a creak.

"So much so that you didn't even have the decency to attend her funeral?" She fisted her hand on her hip. "Didn't even bother to pay your last respects?"

"I couldn't! They've been following me continuously."

So he led them here? She couldn't help looking at the front windows.

He followed her gaze and rushed to the window, jerking the curtains closed all the way. "I need you to give me ten thousand dollars."

She let out a snort. "Do you think I just keep that kind of money lying around?"

"You have it. I know you do." He towered over her.

"Not in cash, and not here." Maybe she should try reasoning. "Kipp, paying them isn't going to make everything okay. Jolie's dead. Murdered. Stabbed multiple times." Bile nearly choked her, but she forced herself to continue. "If these people are the ones responsible, by not going to the police, you're letting them off the hook. You're helping them get away with murder."

The muscles in his jaw flinched. "Don't you think I know that? That it makes me feel like I'm no better than pond scum? But I can't do anything if I'm dead."

"Paying them won't bring her back, or give her justice." Keep calm, keep him talking, that was her plan. Her only choice, really.

"Justice? You think they care about justice? They don't. All they care about is their money."

She inched away from him, slowly. "And then what? You pay them off and everything's okay? They back off?" She shook her head. "What about Jolie?"

"She's dead. As hard as that is for me to accept, I can't change that." He scratched his fingers through his hair.

"And you're okay with paying *your sister's* murderers?" She took another slow step backward.

"If it keeps me alive, yes!" He closed the distance between them and gripped her shoulder. "Now, where's the money?"

Pressing her lips tightly, she ran through her options. Should she give him the money and send him on his way, try to outrun him and make it down the hall to the bedroom where her other phone sat on her nightstand or try to reason with him to call the police himself? She studied his expression, his eyes. Strike out option three — he wouldn't turn himself into the police. The tired muscles in her legs told her trying to outrun him wasn't really a choice, either. That left option one — give him the money and hope he left.

"I don't have it here." His eyes turned dark, dangerous, deadly. "But I can write you a check."

"And you'll call the police as soon as I leave and have them pick me up at the bank."

She prayed someone on the other end of her phone had already made the call. "That's a chance you'll have to take." *Lord, I need a little divine intervention.* "Take it or leave it. It's the best I can offer."

Spencer's heartbeat kicked into overdrive. From the minute an operator had patched the call through to his cell phone, he'd listened to Felicia try to talk down Kipp Landry. He'd called the sheriff, then jumped in his truck. A sheen of sweat coated his palms, and tightening his grip on the steering wheel didn't help matters. Why was traffic so congested today, of all days?

"Let go of me." Felicia's voice sounded strong, but her words sent icy chills down Spencer's spine. Eight minutes had passed since he'd called the police, but he still didn't hear any sirens or see any cruisers racing down the road.

"Are you going to give me the money or not?"

Spencer held his breath as he waited for Felicia's answer. What was happening? Did Kipp have her in a choke hold? *Lord, please let her be okay.*

"Fine. Let me get my checkbook."

Spencer let out a pent-up breath. He had to get there fast. What if he failed her, too? Guilt and fear had him pressing the accelerator harder.

Two more turns and he'd be at her apartment.

"Where's your checkbook?" Kipp's voice gained a raw edge.

"In my purse. On the table there." Was that a crack in her voice?

Father, please watch over Felicia. Give her strength and wisdom.

"You stay there, I'll get your purse."

If the car in front of him would just move. Yes! The sedan veered left, and Spencer punched the gas. Might be a good idea for a cop to clock him speeding — nothing like arriving with the cavalry, even if it'd land him in murky water.

"Yes, that's it." Felicia still sounded strong, but what did Spencer expect? She'd been through so much in the past year, being the victim of extortion would be a walk in the park for her. She'd hold her own with Kipp Landry.

One more turn, not even a block away. *Hold on, Felicia, I'm coming.* He shoved away the thought of why he was so afraid, not wanting to analyze his emotions right now. No time. A siren whirred, and his heartbeat raced.

"Just make the check out to cash." Kipp's voice held an impatient edge. They could probably hear the sirens, too.

"The bank will question that on such a large amount."

Why did she have to be so logical? Couldn't she just write the check and get him out the door?

"Make it out to me, then. Hurry."

A trash truck blocked the way. Spencer slammed on his brakes and slapped the side of his fist against the steering wheel. The siren screamed louder, drawing closer.

"Here you go."

Spencer pressed on the horn. His thumb caught on the wire of his headset, snatching the earbud into his lap. He fumbled to replace it.

The truck moved. Spencer wove around.

Silence filled his ear. He grabbed the cell phone and glanced at the LCD screen — the call hadn't been disconnected. Yanking out the earpiece, he held the phone tightly against his ear as he whipped onto the complex's street and skidded to a stop in the parking lot beside the sheriff's car.

Scrambling out of the truck, he rounded the building, groping as he slipped the open phone into its belt latch. The door to her apartment stood ajar. Spencer burst into the living room. "Where is he?" Spencer all but yelled.

Sitting on the couch across from the sheriff, Felicia shook her head. "H-he's gone."

Spencer couldn't have missed him by more than a few minutes at most. "Did you get him?" he asked Sheriff Theriot as he lowered himself to the couch and pulled Felicia into the safe circle of his embrace.

Thank You, Father.

"I'm okay." She pushed free of his hug and gave him a nervous smile. "Really, I'm more mad than upset."

"I've dispatched deputies to all branches of Felicia's bank." Sheriff Theriot held a pencil over his notebook. "Kipp Landry doesn't have a checking or savings account, so he'll have to try to cash the check at one of the branches of her bank."

Spencer focused on Felicia. "I heard most of the conversation. Did he hurt you?"

She shook her head. "Just grabbed my wrist." She lifted her hand. "Not even a mark."

Just the thought of his hands on her sent more anger pumping through Spencer's veins. He forced himself to take a deep breath. No, he wouldn't let his emotions dictate his actions. Not again. Instead, he hugged Felicia tighter. It felt so natural for her to be in his arms.

An electronic beep filled the room.

She pulled her cell phone from her pocket, then smiled at him. "We're still connected."

Sure enough, his phone, still open, held the connection. Something told Spencer they were linked in more ways than an open phone line.

His heartbeat wouldn't slow, not when he'd come so close to losing her tonight. And because he'd been so scared, what did that say about his feelings for her?

EIGHT

"To be honest, he looked like a druggie needing a fix." Felicia took a sip of her iced tea and studied Sheriff Theriot over the rim of the glass. The sheriff had radioed several times over with his deputies, but there was still no sign of Kipp at any of the bank locations.

"And he didn't mention any names of these loan sharks?"

Felicia set the drink down with an echoing *thunk*. "No, he did not." She'd answered the same questions for the better part of an hour, and her patience was close to snapping. She shoved to her feet and grabbed her cane. "If there's nothing else, I'd like to start getting my apartment back in order."

Sheriff Theriot stood as well, pocketing his trusty notebook. "That's all for now. If you find anything missing, you'll need to let me know. I went ahead and called Luc for you. He should be here any minute."

Her muscles locked. "You did what?"

"Called Luc for you. Thought I'd save you some time."

"I had no intention of calling my brother just yet." She narrowed her eyes, pushing down the flaming words burning her tongue. "It's none of his business. You had no right to call him, Sheriff." Now she'd have to deal with him bullying her to move home, just when he'd started to back off. His threat of packing her up if there was any further sign of violence rang in her ears.

"I'm sorry if I overstepped. I just thought you'd want him here. At least until Kipp is caught." The sheriff shook his head and ambled to the door.

Good manners wouldn't allow her to let him leave without a soft word. "*Merci,* Sheriff."

His cell phone rang. "Sheriff Theriot."

Felicia stood silent, watching the tense lines of his body language and unabashedly eavesdropping.

"Great. Bring him to the station for questioning. I'll meet you there." He shut his phone and grinned at her. "They found Kipp at the bank branch in Abbeville. My deputy stopped him as soon as he came in the door. We'll keep the check as evidence of his extortion." He opened the door. "I'll let you know what the status is."

The door closed with an empty thud. She took in the shambles of the room, let out a small huff, then lifted a cushion and put it back on the Queen Anne chair.

"I'll help."

Startled, she turned. Spence had already begun shoving couch pillows back to their places. How could she have forgotten he was still there? "You don't have to help me. I'm not an invalid, you know."

"I never implied you were. I'm just offering to help you."

She slammed the phone back to its rightful place on the end table. "I'm sick of people thinking I can't do for myself. Or make decisions."

"Are you talking about me, here, or Luc?"

He had her there. But did he have to be the voice of reason? She fisted her hands on her hips. "More Luc and the sheriff than you. But I'm not really happy with you right now, either."

"Why's that?" He set the stack of magazines on the coffee table.

"Because you confuse me."

His hands froze as he slowly straightened.

Had she just said that aloud? Good gravy, what was it with her mouth lately?

"How do I confuse you?"

107

"Forget it."

"No, I want to know." He laid a hand on her arm.

Little pulses of heat shot up her arm and tugged against her heart. That she felt that way annoyed her all the more. She jerked her arm from his. "Don't touch me. I'm tired of people grabbing me."

Shadows marched across his features as he dropped his hand. "I didn't grab you, Felicia."

What was wrong with her? Why was she so snappy all of a sudden? "I'm sorry, Spence. I didn't mean to bite your head off, yes?"

"Sit down for a minute." He stared into her eyes and sat on the couch he'd just straightened. "Please." The softness of his tone nearly unraveled her tenuous hold on her emotions.

She dropped to the chair.

"What do you mean I confuse you?"

"You treat me like I'm special to you, awaken all kinds of feelings in me I thought were dead, then you push me away, only to run to my rescue when you think I'm in trouble. It's conflicting and confusing." Oh, she was going for the big score here, baring her emotional train wreck right out in the open.

"I — I . . ."

She held up a hand. "I don't want anything from you, Spence, but honesty. I've had enough lies to fill my lifetime. But I can't let you play with my emotions, either. I need you to shoot straight with me."

"I'm sorry."

For a moment she stared at him. After everything she'd admitted, all he could offer was an apology? She stood. "That's it? You're sorry? No, I'm the one who's sorry. Do me a favor and just stay away from me."

He rushed to his feet. "Felicia."

"No. Don't use that soft tone with me. I can't deal with . . . *this* right now." She spun around, her leg muscles cramping at the sudden movement.

He was at her side in an instant, holding her elbow and supporting her. So close, his breath fanned her temple. "I care about you, but I shouldn't." His words were a caress against her skin.

Her heartbeat raced. "Why shouldn't you?"

She could drown in his eyes, so full of depth and emotion. She laid a hand on his face. Stubble brushed against her palm. "Why shouldn't you care about me?" She had to know.

He straightened but kept his hold under

her elbow. "Because I don't deserve you."

What? "That's the stupidest thing I've ever heard you say, Spencer Bertrand. You sound like a *cooyon*."

"It's the truth." Pain glimmered in his eyes.

"Why would you think such an absurd thing?"

He backed away, shaking his head. "Please don't ask me to explain."

Felicia blinked to hold in the tears. "Fine. That's it. I can't do this. I want you to leave." She pointed to the door with a trembling finger. "Now." If he didn't leave now, she'd break down. The last thing she wanted was for him to hold her again out of pity.

He took a step toward her. "Fel—"

"No." She pressed her hand against her mouth and shook her head. "Just go. Leave."

"I can't while you're so upset."

"I'm fine. Or, I will be as soon as you go." Tears burned the back of her eyelids.

"No, you aren't."

"Spence, please." Why did her voice have to hitch like that? She sounded desperate. Weak. It infuriated her to no end. Hadn't she put away her weaknesses and surged on with independence?

"Okay." His stare wouldn't break from

hers. The thudding of her heart measured every second. "Would you like me to talk to Luc?"

"Fine. Tell him I'm hunky-dory and don't need him, or anyone else for that matter, to run to my rescue."

"He'll want to see you."

"I don't want to see him, you, anybody. Not now."

Spence hesitated, then gave a jerky nod before he left the apartment.

Felicia dropped to the couch, burying her face in her hands. He didn't want her — said he shouldn't care about her. What possible reason could anyone have for such nonsense? It had to be an excuse. She was the *cooyon.* Letting herself think they might be able to have something special. But she'd been wrong.

Rejection left a bitter taste in her mouth.

The woman would drive him insane. Spencer paced in the parking lot, waiting for Luc. He couldn't tell Felicia why he was unworthy of her — she'd never forgive him. He knew it'd be better for her if he did. Then she'd understand it had nothing to do with her, but with him, his past. Still, he couldn't bear the thought of disappointing her, showing her how unworthy he truly was.

Father, I sure could use some of Your wisdom in handling this situation. What do You want me to do?

Luc's truck rambled into the lot and screeched to a stop. "Where's Felicia? How is she?" he asked as he made mean strides to the walkway.

"Madder than a wet hen, right now. I wouldn't advise barging in."

Luc spun and faced him. "What's going on?"

"She was a bit miffed the sheriff called you."

"Why? She knows I'd want to help her."

Spencer kicked a loose rock from the edge of the sidewalk. "I think that's the problem."

"What?"

"She's trying to stake her independence, handle things on her own."

"There's a killer on the loose, and it could very well be Kipp Landry. Didn't that occur to her?" He shook his head. "Do you know she went to the jazz club looking for Sadie? What's she trying to do?"

Spencer held up his hands in mock surrender. "Hey, don't shoot the messenger. They found Kipp and are hauling him in for questioning. I'm just giving you fair warning she's stewing in there and might snap at you." He lowered his voice. "She went looking for Sadie?"

"A friend called and told me she'd been in the club asking for Sadie. She doesn't get how serious this is."

"I can't believe she'd do something so foolish." Spencer's heart hammered. What on this blessed green earth had she been thinking?

Luc's eyes narrowed. "Why are you here, anyway? Aren't you supposed to be at the center?"

Just what he didn't need — confession time with her brother. Her very big brother who took protectiveness to a whole new level.

"I'm sure the sheriff told you Felicia called the center and I called him."

"Yeah. And?"

"Well, I was worried about her."

Luc's eyes narrowed into tiny slits. "Is there something going on I should know about?"

Spencer fought the urge to squirm under his scrutiny. "Not really."

"What's that supposed to mean?"

"It just means there are some issues Felicia and I are working out. Privately." He stood tall, measuring up Luc Trahan.

A grin spread across Luc's face. "You like her, don't you?"

Spencer's blood pressure spiked. "I do, but you don't need to worry about that."

"Why not? What's wrong with my sister?"

"Not a thing. That's the problem. She's too good for me."

Luc smiled again. "No argument there, Pastor. She's too good for most of us. But that won't matter to her." He cocked his head. "Is she not interested in you?"

He so didn't want to have this discussion, especially with her big brother. "I think she could be, but that's not the point."

"Then what is?"

A chirping sounded. Luc snatched his cell phone off his belt clip. Spencer let out a long breath. Saved by the phone.

He took two steps and leaned against the building, affording Luc some privacy while also giving himself a few minutes to think. Should he tell Felicia the truth now, before this thing between them went any further, and let her hate him? Or, should he just walk away from her with no explanation? Which would hurt her the least?

Telling her the truth.

But that'd hurt him. He didn't know if he could stand having her look at him with disappointment or disgust.

"Look, Mom's just checked herself into a rehab clinic in Covington. I need to go

114

check on her, but I don't want to leave Felicia." Luc's face was pale.

"Go check on your mother. I'll stay here and keep an eye on Felicia. Kipp's in custody, so he's no longer a threat." Like Spencer would leave her alone?

"I need to tell her about Mom."

"Hey, it's your funeral."

Luc strode to Felicia's door. Spencer trailed, keeping a safe distance. He didn't want to witness a family argument, but had no other choice but to follow.

"I don't need you here," Felicia said as she opened the door.

"Are you just trying to put yourself in the line of fire?" Luc's hands fisted at his side.

"It's my business if I do, yes?"

"You went looking for Sadie! Come on, *Boo,* you have no business doing that. Let the police do their job."

"Jolie was my best friend, Luc. You and I both know from experience that they have to do things a certain way, which sometimes gets in the way of the truth." Her voice hitched.

"But you aren't a detective. You need to let this go." Luc framed the doorway, invading his sister's space. "If you keep doing insane things, you'll have to come back home where you'll be safe."

"I'm not a child, Luc." Her voice rose an octave.

"Then stop acting like one!"

"Just go. Leave me alone." She slammed the door. The click of a dead bolt echoed across the courtyard.

Luc shook his head and knocked again. "Open the door. I have something to tell you. About Mom."

The wait felt like forever as he leaned against the wall. Spencer's stomach cramped. He hated confrontations like this. Had seen enough, been through enough, to last a lifetime.

Luc rapped his knuckles against the door. "C'mon, Felicia. I'm serious."

Still no answer.

He turned from the door and caught sight of Spencer. "She's probably gone in the back where she can't hear. Tuning me out."

Spencer nodded. What could he say?

"I need to check on Mom. Will you tell Felicia where we are when she calms down?"

"Sure." Great, he'd be the bearer of bad news again.

"*Merci,* Pastor." Luc headed to the parking lot.

Spencer fell into step alongside him. "I'll be praying for your mother." He patted Luc's shoulder.

"I appreciate that. Tell Felicia I'll call her after I've seen about Mom."

Luc peeled out of the parking lot, tossing loose gravel onto the sidewalk. Spencer headed to Felicia's apartment. Maybe she'd cooled off some by now. He hoped so. He felt a little like Daniel being tossed into the lions' den.

Wrapped up in his thoughts, he clipped a person with his shoulder. Glancing up, Spencer stared into the face of a tired-looking young woman. "Excuse me," he muttered.

"Same," she replied, continuing her trek down the walkway.

Something about her voice sounded familiar to him. What was it? He glanced over his shoulder. She wasn't a member of his congregation, that much he knew. Had she visited, perhaps?

Felicia's door swung open, and she stepped onto the sidewalk, her cane in her right hand and a yard-size trash bag in the other. She dropped the bag when her eyes lit on him. "What're you still doing here?"

"I talked to Luc."

She peered over his shoulder. "Is he making plans to come in and scoop me back home? Didn't you tell him the sheriff has Kipp?"

Obviously not enough time had passed to cool her ire.

"Uh, Felicia, I need to tell you something."

Anger scurried from her eyes. "What's wrong?" She leaned against the door frame.

"Luc received a call. Your mother's checked herself into a rehab clinic."

"What?" The cane tumbled to the concrete. "Where? When?"

Spencer slowly handed her cane back to her, careful not to be obvious in taking care of her. "All I know is she's at a place in Covington, and Luc said he'd call you once he checked in on her."

Her blue eyes shimmered with tears. "It's all my fault. Luc warned me she'd begun drinking again after I moved back here, but I didn't listen." She shook her head. "No, I had to be Ms. Independence and think only of myself. Selfish, selfish, selfish." Her last words were barely audible.

He couldn't take her beating herself up. Reaction and instinct kicked in. He wrapped his arm around her shoulders and drew her into the curve of his arm. Her entire body trembled. He planted a kiss on her temple, ignoring the little voice in his head warning him to keep his distance.

But as she clung to him tighter than ever

before, Spencer had a sneaking suspicion
his heart would drown out the alarms.

NINE

Wasn't there a rule somewhere in the universe that mornings were milder, calmer in the South? Wasn't that why people referred to New Orleans as the Big Easy? If no such rule existed, it should.

Unfortunately, Felicia had a morning as dense as the lily pads on the bayou. Physical therapy had been a cakewalk compared to the visit with her mother. The lamenting, the crying, the theatrics, not to mention the free guilt trip . . . all wore Felicia slap out. Yet she still had another stop to make.

Two Mardi Gras masks covered the entryway into the sheriff's office. She yanked the door open with a weight in her heart despite the revelry of the decorations. After asking the dispatcher, Missy, to see the sheriff and being told to have a seat, Felicia checked her cell phone again — no missed calls. Why hadn't Sheriff Theriot called last night and given an update on Kipp?

120

And why hadn't she heard from Spence?

No, she wouldn't wonder about that. He'd made his intentions, or lack thereof, very clear. She'd remove him from her mind, once and for all.

Shame her heart wouldn't comply.

The door whisked open, pulling in the nippy February air. A deputy led a hand-cuffed man through the swinging door. Felicia scowled as they disappeared around the corner. But once she'd realized what she'd done, a chill deeper than the temperature settled in the pit of her stomach. Had she really become so hardened against criminals that she couldn't comprehend forgiveness? The thought made her shudder. She'd have to work on letting go of such animosity.

"Felicia."

She snapped up her head and struggled to stand. "Sheriff Theriot."

"What can I help you with?"

"Kipp Landry? Jolie's murder?"

He let out a weary sigh and opened the swinging door. "*Allons* back to my office."

She exerted care with each heavy step until she dropped into a chair in his office. "You said you'd call me. About Kipp."

The sheriff sat behind his desk, the wooden chair legs creaking against the weight. "We have two options here, Felicia. One, release him and put a tail on him. See if he leads us to these loan sharks. Or two, keep him here with the extortion charge and maybe never learn who killed Jolie."

"He hasn't given up their names?"

"Nope. Says he's too scared."

"Can't you make him tell you?"

"You know as well as I do that you can't make somebody cough up a name if they don't want to."

She crossed her arms over her chest and glared. "You seemed to do quite well when you were intimidating my brother, yes?"

His face flushed. "C'mon, Felicia. I was just doing my job. Luc understands that."

She knew it, too. "Why didn't you call and tell me this?"

He squirmed and avoided eye contact.

"You called Luc again, didn't you?"

"Look, I know Kipp scared you and all, but I really think we have a better chance to get to the truth by letting him out and following him."

"He didn't scare me. He made me furious." She stomped to her feet. "So you confided in Luc to get him to urge me not to press charges against Kipp for his extortion."

He stood. "We're running out of clues on

the case, Felicia. I'll use whatever I have in order to get a break."

"Including me?"

"I don't think you're in any danger."

The image of Kipp's enraged face blipped across her mental radar. The sheriff might not be right on that danger issue. "Have you considered Kipp could've killed Jolie? People do murder their kin." Like Grandfather's killer.

"We did. His alibi for the time of death holds."

"What alibi?"

"He was at the casino, at the blackjack table. The manager verified that."

"Who could be involved with the loan sharks and lying for him, yes? The involvement of the casino in my grandfather's case proved the unreliability of those people."

Sheriff Theriot shook his head. "Security tapes don't lie."

Figured he'd have a thick-as-Spanish-moss alibi. "What about Sadie Thompson? Our neighbor heard yelling and identified Sadie at the scene of the crime."

"She's been cleared because the timing isn't right. And, she has an alibi." He scowled. "I understand you went looking for Sadie. You're bordering on interfering in a police investigation, Felicia."

"There's no law that says I can't talk to people, yes?" She blew off the implied warning, opting to appeal to his emotions instead. "Jolie was my best friend, Sheriff. Our neighbor saw Sadie and heard her yelling at Jolie."

"The time of death was after Sadie left. The coroner confirmed it."

"She could be lying about when she left. Sadie's not exactly the most trustworthy person in Lagniappe, you know."

He gave her a soft smile. "Don't you think we verified her alibi?"

"But is the verifier honest?"

"I'd say the preacher of our church is pretty honest."

Felicia snorted. "Our preacher? *Sadie* was with our preacher? Whatever for?"

"I'm not at liberty to say."

"Just because someone's a preacher doesn't make them righteous." Or above playing with someone's emotions. Felicia pressed her lips together, shoving out Spence's image.

"Good point." The sheriff sighed. "Look, we're checking out every lead we have. But right now, my gut tells me to go with following Kipp and see where it goes."

"What about Wesley? Is he still a suspect in your book?"

"Right now, we're focusing our efforts on Kipp, but we'll consider all evidence."

Would justice ever be served for Jolie? And what about Luc? Would letting Kipp walk make her brother demand she move back home, especially with all that was happening with their mother?

"I really wish you hadn't called Luc, Bubba."

Sheepishness darkened his face, despite the glow his red hair cast from the overhead lights. "I didn't get to talk to him, if that helps any. I left a message on his voice mail."

Maybe she had a shot at keeping her independence. "What'd you say on the message?"

"Just that I wanted his opinion on the extortion charges."

Yes! "When he calls back, you can just tell him the situation's been handled."

"Has it?" He arched a brow.

She let out a sigh. Either take a chance on solving Jolie's murder and silencing Luc's threat to move her back home or stand on principle and risk having the goals she'd worked so hard to attain ripped out from under her. What a choice. "Yes. I won't press the extortion charges."

Lord, did You have to make her so beautiful

from the inside out?

Spencer stared across the center, his focus on Felicia in spite of himself. His eyes had a mind of their own.

But I tell You that anyone who looks at a woman lustfully has already committed adultery with her in his heart.

Did that Scripture apply if he wasn't married? Wait a minute, he didn't feel lust for her. He felt affection for her, yes, but not lust. So that Scripture didn't apply at all.

How about *"If your right eye causes you to sin, gouge it out and throw it away. It is better for you to lose one part of your body than for your whole body to be thrown into hell"?* Was his focus on Felicia and not the case causing him to sin? Should he be focusing more on protecting the center?

Nothing but silence answered him.

Felicia waved, her arm flailing. He rushed to her station.

"I'm sorry, Winnie, but we had to notify the police of your calls. I'm sure you have no intention on acting violently toward your ex, but we have a moral obligation to report your comments." Felicia wrapped the cord around her pointer finger.

Spencer grabbed the secondary headset and plugged into the call.

"Can't believe you'd stoop so low. This is

what I get for calling a Christian hotline. And I thought we could be friends."

"No matter what kind of hotline you called, the operator is still obligated to report such threats."

"I don't believe you. It's only because you're part of those do-gooders."

Spencer activated the microphone on his headset. "Winnie, this is Pastor Bertrand and —"

"She switched my call to you? I don't believe that piece of . . ."

The disconnection popped, as if she'd slammed the phone down. Spencer tossed the headset onto the desk while Felicia dropped her head. "She's right. We don't normally report such things to the police."

Spencer tucked a knuckle under her chin and lifted her face to his. "That was before Jolie was murdered. We have to put safeguards in place. Don't you feel guilty over this, Felicia."

She jerked away from his touch. "That woman has nothing to do with Jolie's murder."

"No, but it's made me realize I need to tighten procedures around here." His heart raced as she met his stare. "To protect y'all."

"But word will get out on the street that we're snitches, and nobody will call in. How can we help them then?"

"We have to trust that God will send the people here who need us. Who we can help."

He met her gaze.

Big mistake.

Longing for what could be shoved the air from his lungs.

She nodded. "I know you're right, but it's discouraging. For the callers, I mean."

He could detect the disappointment hovering in her tone. Just about the center, or was there more?

A sinking feeling sat in the pit of his gut. After Frank had been killed, she'd kept everyone at arm's length, not willing to take the chance to be hurt again. He'd watched her rebuild her life on her own terms. Now she looked at him with something else. Something beyond the friendship they'd forged.

He met her inquiring stare, the one that pinned him to the spot. Waiting for him to say something. "God will work through us, regardless of the guidelines we work within."

She let out a soft sigh. Obviously not the response she'd been looking for. "I —"

Her phone rang. She gave him a half smile and lifted the receiver.

He couldn't resist squeezing her shoulder before trudging back to his office. The need to put his face to the floor pulled his steps faster. The time had come to do some real seeking from the Father.

TEN

A smile tickled Felicia's lips when she passed through the curtain of metallic gold and purple and entered the center. Signs decorated the door, announcing the upcoming Mardi Gras Masquerade Ball. A Lagniappe tradition.

She stowed her belongings and slid into her station. Tonight would be a good night. She'd help people, pray with and for them and her spirit would be one of tranquility.

"You look happy."

Felicia twisted to find Spence hovering behind her chair. Her heart did a funny flip, but she sternly ordered it to stay still. She would respect his wishes to just be friends. After all, wasn't that better than nothing? Now that she had no more smoldering ties to the past, she'd allow herself to live fully again.

Even if it wasn't with the man who'd already slipped under her exterior.

Regret pushed away, Felicia smiled. "I am."

He brushed at his jeans. "Uh, the city events planner came by today and posted the signs for the ball."

"I noticed. Looks like it's going to be another fun time this year. Luc's band will play." And maybe Sadie would show up. Felicia could possibly strike up a conversation, see where it led. There had to be some reason Sadie had shown up at the apartment, and Felicia was determined to find out what that reason was. Sure, the sheriff said Sadie had an alibi, but the question still burning in Felicia's mind was why Sadie had shown up, yelling, in the first place.

"Yeah, that's what the planner said. She's encouraging everybody to attend."

"You've gone in years past. Aren't you planning on going this year?" She certainly wouldn't miss the ball. It was *the* event of the year in south Louisiana. Of course, Frank had been her escort last year. She suppressed the thought. No more sadness hiding in the dark recesses of her heart. God would grant her contentment if she focused on Him.

"I'd like to."

She quirked a single brow. "But?"

"I don't want to go alone."

131

"Don't be silly. There'll be tons of people you know. I bet your entire congregation will attend."

"Exactly." His brow creased.

What was going on with him? He acted odd, very odd. Maybe because of the tension between them? She should pull up her big-girl pants and bite the bullet. Let him know it was okay for him to not want to pursue a relationship with her. "Spence, I don—"

"Felicia, will you go to the ball with me?"

Her unspoken words turned foreign on her tongue. Her jaw dropped. Mercy, had he just asked her to be his date? Hope fluttered in her chest.

Uncertainty danced in his beautiful eyes. "I know I've been giving you mixed signals. I'm sorry. I spent a lot of time in prayer last night and today and I'd rea—"

"Yes." Her heart hammered her ribs. So the Holy Spirit had grappled with Spence too. How ironic. No, how God.

He blinked. "What?"

"Yes, I'll go to the ball with you."

"I'm glad." His smile brightened the entire center.

"Felicia, there's something I need to te—"

Sheriff Theriot's grand entrance interrupted Spence. The creaking of his service belt marked the lawman's quick stride, and his eyes were narrowed behind the lenses of his glasses. Something had clearly unsettled the man. "Pastor Bertrand, I need to have a word with you."

"Is there a problem, Sheriff?"

Felicia stood, putting every inch into her height. Had they found Jolie's killer? Had they found a link to the center and come to close it down?

"Why didn't you tell us about your past?" The sheriff rested his hands on his holsters.

Spence's Adam's apple bobbed. His eyes darted about the center. Every operator bolted into some activity, as if they weren't listening. For once, the phones sat silent.

"Why didn't you tell me you'd been in prison for assault?"

Spencer kept his gaze on Felicia's face, which had turned a most interesting shade of ashen. Her eyes widened and a range of raw emotion shimmered in their Caribbean-blue depths.

Pain. Disappointment. Betrayal.

Spencer's heart plummeted. His worst fear had been realized.

"Pastor?" The sheriff drummed his fingers against his leather holster.

"Why don't we go into my office?"

"Wh-why, indeed?" Felicia stammered. Big tears found their way down her cheeks. "Don't let me stop you." She snatched up her cane, drew her purse strap over her shoulder and slammed the chair under the desk. "I believe I'm taking the night off, *Pastor*."

"Felicia, wait." He grabbed a gentle hold on her arm.

She jerked herself free of his grasp, piercing him with a glare of pure ice. "Don't. Just don't." Pain shot through his veins from her cold response. "I think you have an important conversation waiting on you."

Without another word, she stalked to the door.

Look back, please look back.

But she didn't. Not even a glance over her shoulder as she stormed from the center.

A good amount of self-loathing joined the dose Felicia had already given him. He ached to run after her.

"Pastor?"

Alas, he'd have to find her later and try to defend his past. For now, he'd have to explain to the sheriff. Then the operators. And he'd have to call the church elders and tell them. More than likely, his congregation would call for his replacement.

He could almost hear the rumble as his carefully constructed life crashed down on his shoulders.

He was helpless to stop the destruction.

What a *cooyon* she was!

How could he? Encouraging her to forgive the person who murdered Frank, to give men in prison the benefit of the doubt — yeah, she understood perfectly now. Setting her up.

Fat tears marred Felicia's vision as she punched in the speed-dial number for her driver. Just when she'd made strides to reconsider her animosity toward criminals, now she found out the one man who'd hit her soft part was one. And for a violent crime, too!

She leaned against the rough exterior of the center. The Mardi Gras decorations fluttered in the late February breeze. The moon danced across the sky, as if it hadn't a care in the world.

Lucky moon.

After snapping out her request to the driver and closing the phone, Felicia glowered at the announcement of the ball mocking her from the adjacent storefront. With a renewed resentment, she marched across the walkway and snatched the notice from the window, crumbling the paper into a tight wad.

How did a preacher go to prison? Especially for assault. The mere concept boggled her mind.

The wind, swirling like black ink in murky water, lifted the hair from her nape. She shivered.

Forgive and act; deal with each man according to all he does, since you know his heart (for you alone know the hearts of all men).

Where'd that Scripture come from? Felicia rested her head against the wall. What did it mean? Was the Holy Spirit leading her somewhere?

The driver pulled to the curb, jumped out and held open the back door. "Everything okay, Ms. Felicia?"

No, nothing was okay, and she didn't know if it'd ever be okay again. This was all too much to take. She needed inner peace, spiritual peace. Slipping into the leather seat, she stared at her driver. "Can you take me to church?"

"Lagniappe Community?"

Her church, the one she and Luc had attended with Grandfather for as long as she could remember. But today, her spirit yearned for something different, a change. She shook her head. "No, I'd like to go to

Vermilion Parish Fellowship."

Spence's church. How fitting.

The driver flashed her a confused look before shutting the door, but didn't argue. Felicia leaned back against the cool leather. This could be a trip in vain. If Spence was at the center, chances were there was no one at the church. Being so small, it might even be locked up. Still, something inside led her to Spence's church.

Her cell phone chirped. She glanced at the caller ID. Luc. Great. Just what she didn't need right now. She pressed the button to send the call directly to voice mail and glanced out the window.

Even though the grounds were outside the city limits of Lagniappe, the drive to the small community church took less than twenty minutes. But as her anger started to dim, twenty minutes was time enough for Felicia to struggle with the concept of having judged Spence. Without facts, without explanation.

Nestled in the bayou with cypress trees coated in Spanish moss providing a natural archway, the building had seen its share of elements. Paint cracked and peeled. The concrete steps were weathered and split. The planks creaked as Felicia made her way to the entrance, and a lone glass pane adorned the unlocked white door.

Wind shoved against her as Felicia yanked on the door, and dry leaves followed her inside to dance over the trodden wood floor of the foyer.

She hesitated, her heart pounding, and let her eyes adjust to the darkness. A long red carpet led the way to the front, splitting the rows of pews in half. The altar held four lit candles. Flames flickered in the breeze. Felicia eased to the front row and took a seat.

Wind howled outside, causing the stained-glass windows to tremble. Felicia wrapped her arms around her middle and rocked. Had she become so cynical, so judgmental that she was as harsh as a cold winter wind? Without attention to her legs, she knelt at the altar.

Time stood still as she conversed with God. Leaning on Him, listening to Him minister to her heart.

The back door to the church opened with a crash.

Felicia started and tried to jump to her feet. Her leg muscles locked and she swayed.

Spence was there in an instant, steadying her. "Whoa. Let's get you sitting down." He led her to the pew and sat beside her.

"How'd you know where I was?"

He gave her a sheepish grin. "I called Luc."

"But I didn't answer his call."

"Yeah, and he wasn't too happy about that. There's still a killer out there, and you should be more careful." He slipped a lock of her hair behind her ear.

The gesture felt intimate, and heat fanned her face. Better to steer clear of these emotions. At least while she still couldn't discern what she felt. She leaned away from him. "So, how'd he know I was here?"

"When you didn't answer, he got worried and called your driver."

She was surrounded by meddling men. "I'm going to hire my own driver, a person whom Luc doesn't keep on the payroll," she mumbled.

"Don't be too hard on either of them. They're just concerned for you. We all are."

Really? Hmm. She crossed her arms over her chest. "I'm quite capable of handling myself, yes?"

"I know that. But you aren't my baby sister, either."

She sat silent for a moment, digesting the emotion in his tone. And waited.

Spence gave a huffy sigh and leaned back against the pew. "You know, I've never sat here and stared at the altar. Interesting view, isn't it?"

"Mmm-hmm." While she'd be willing to listen, she wouldn't make his sharing any easier, either. He had, after all, kept this vital piece of his past from her, even though he'd known how she struggled with what had happened to her grandfather and Frank, and how she abhorred violence.

"Speaking of little sisters . . ."

She twisted to face him and arched an eyebrow.

"I need to explain. Will you hear me out before you say anything?"

"Yes."

"Okay." He took a deep breath. "I had a little sister. Carrie. Sweet and innocent. Eight years younger than me." His face took on a faraway gaze. "She was the sunshine in my life. Our father died before she was born. I helped my mom in raising Carrie from birth. She was a little miracle."

Heart thumping, Felicia nodded. Babies were truly a blessing from God.

"When she was sixteen, she got a weekend job at a local McDonald's just out of Alexandria."

Felicia realized she didn't know where Spence was from, or why he came to Lagniappe. All CoCo had told her about her preacher was that he was from Louisiana and, after seminary, had wanted to move to a small community. Felicia'd never questioned more. Maybe she should have.

"Carrie was scheduled for closing one Saturday night, so we didn't expect her home until after midnight. I was going to LSU-S, but came home every weekend to help Mom and Carrie." He leaned forward and held his head in his hands. "I'll never forget that night. One o'clock rolled around, and Carrie wasn't home. Mom woke me up and asked me to go looking for her. I knew the route she'd take from work. We were concerned because the old clunker Carrie drove was famous for breaking down. Throwing the timing belt." He shook his head. "I meant to get her a better car once I had a job."

Felicia's hands trembled. Her muscles tensed. She knew he was about to tell her something horrible.

"I drove the route and never saw her car. When I pulled into the parking lot of McDonald's, I spotted her car right off. Parked in the back, almost behind the Dumpster." He sat upright, his focus on the cross over the altar. "No one was around. The lights were out in the building, so I went to her car to check things out."

Pain distorted his handsome features. Felicia laid a hand on his shoulder, and he turned his intense gaze to her face. "I found her, Felicia. Naked in the back seat. Still." Tears spilled down his face. "She was dead. I checked for a pulse, laid my head on her chest to try to hear a heartbeat. Nothing. She was gone." His body shook as he sobbed.

Felicia's own eyes filled with tears as her heart constricted. She inched forward, wrapping her arm around his shoulders.

Spence wiped his face and took in a long breath. "The police came. So did the coroner. Reports came back. She'd been raped and strangled. Time of death not even an hour before I found her. An hour." He twisted to stare at Felicia. "I was at home sleeping while someone raped and strangled my sister. My sweet Carrie." Rage held his tears in place.

"That's not your fault." Felicia's voice cracked.

"Maybe not." He ran a hand over his shaggy hair, composing himself. "Weeks later, the police arrested a suspect. A man who was on parole for a sexual assault charge." Spence clenched his jaw, the muscles popping. "Trial date was set. Mom and I geared up to attend, no matter how painful."

Felicia swallowed. Such pain he'd endured. How awful. She knew — been there, done that, never wanted to experience anything like it again.

"Three days before trial, the district attorney called Mom and told her they had to drop the charges as their case wouldn't stand up in court."

"What?" Shock and outrage stiffened Felicia's spine.

"Yeah. Exactly what I said." He leaned back against the pew. "Apparently, the police had illegally searched the guy's room. The evidence they recovered linking him to Carrie's murder couldn't be used in court because the police had failed to get a proper warrant."

"Oh, Spence. How horrible."

"Yeah. So, her killer would go free. Nothing we could do about it." He let out an exaggerated breath and stood, leaning against the railing of the altar. "I tried to forget. I graduated college with a degree in literature. I tried to move on, get on with my life."

Felicia held her breath, knowing more would come and wanting to know the whole story, but her heart broke for Spence.

"Mom committed suicide the night of my graduation. What a present, huh?"

"Oh, Spence!" Felicia pressed her fingers to her lips. What unimaginable horrors he'd endured. She grabbed her cane, fisting her hand over the handle.

"I went home the next weekend to clean out the house and meet with the real estate agent. I'd made up my mind — I wanted to get away. Far away from the painful memories. I'd finished my business and was heading out of town when I noticed a bar. Even back then, I wasn't much of a drinker. I don't know what made me stop there that day."

He glanced up at the cross, his facial expression unreadable. "Maybe it was God's hand. I still don't know. All I remember is that I sat at the bar and ordered a draft. As I waited, I heard a voice I recognized but couldn't place. I turned on the bar stool and saw him." Spence faced Felicia, meeting her stare. "The man who'd killed Carrie."

ELEVEN

After all these years, telling the story hadn't gotten easier.

Spencer swallowed the lump in his throat. It didn't settle any smoother in his gut. Empathy wrapped Felicia's face. With his last statement, her amazing eyes had widened and her expression turned to one of dread. He could tell she suspected what was coming. Might as well get it all out.

"I stared at him. Openly. I glared, putting all my hatred into the look." Hadn't he felt murderous at that moment?

Within his very spirit. He shivered now at the memory.

"What happened?" Felicia whispered, although there were only the two of them in the church.

"Believe it or not, I turned back to the bar and downed the frosty mug in front of me."

"Then . . . ?"

There always had to be more. He'd asked

145

himself a million times over why he hadn't just gotten up and walked out. But he hadn't. "I heard him laughing. Telling his friends who I was." Shame pressed his head until it hung. "Talking about Carrie like he did . . ."

The laughter tormented Spencer. The names the scum called Carrie. Even now, Spencer clenched his hands into tight fists. "I didn't think. I jumped from the stool and attacked him. Hit him several times. Wrapped my hands around his throat and squeezed."

The memory washed over him like swamp over submerged stumps.

"I kept squeezing, despite him kicking and punching me. I wouldn't let go." Remorse tightened his throat. "His buddies, the guys there with him, tried to pull me off, but I was too full of rage. I never even felt their fists as they tried to pull me off of him."

Felicia let out a whimper and shook her head. Crying for him out of pity or disgust? He tried to tell from her expression but came up with no conclusion.

He had to make her see. Make her understand all of it. "I wanted to kill him just like he killed Carrie. I felt the murderous desire in every part of me. For all practical purposes, I'm a murderer. The urge seared my heart." His voice filled with anger.

Tears streamed down her face. "You didn't kill him, yes?"

He let out a long breath, releasing the anger and self-disgust. "No, I didn't." He shook his head. He had to be totally honest with her, just as she'd asked. "But I wanted to."

"Yet you didn't." She moved closer to him, resting her hand on his forearm.

"Don't you get it? I wanted to. With everything I am."

She tightened her hold on him. "What happened?"

"His eyes bulged. I don't know. Something inside told me to let go. Let go of him and let go of the hatred burning in my chest."

"God."

Spencer nodded. "I'd like to think so." He blinked back the memory. "Anyway, I had the bartender call 911. The police showed up right behind the ambulance. The guy pressed charges. I pled guilty, waiving a trial. Didn't want a plea bargain. Served three years of a five-year sentence."

He let out a ragged breath. He had to continue, had to finish, had to stop being a coward. "God met me in prison and put a call on my life. I left prison and went straight into seminary. Moved here because

I'd met the previous pastor at seminary, and he asked me to replace him."

Pain rolled over him. "My first appointment was in Calcasieu parish. A little church, bigger than Vermilion Community, but not by much. I shared my story with the congregation on my first Sunday in the pulpit. How God could see my heart and use me." He shook his head. "The congregation called for my immediate replacement. I left quietly, started the center and had no intention of going back to preaching. But God had other plans.

"I met with the chair of the pastoral committee by accident." He smiled. "No, by God's intervention. Mr. Fontenot introduced me to the other elders. I told them up front what I'd done, what had happened at my previous church. They agreed to hire me on and gave me the option of when and how to tell my congregation.

"All that to say, I'm on parole for another year." There, he'd said it all. Bared his soul and secrets. The rest was up to her.

And that scared him worse than his first night in prison.

She blinked as if fighting for focus, but her gaze never left his. "You had the chance to kill him, but you didn't. You turned away from him until provoked. It's completely understandable. And you paid for your crime."

"Are you trying to excuse my actions to me or yourself?" He detested how desperate his voice sounded, but he had to be sure of her. He wouldn't let himself cross the hidden emotional line if she couldn't get over his past.

She licked her lips. He straightened and stared at the cross again.

Please, Lord, help me. Give me the strength.

He spread his hands in front of her. They shook with the intensity of his passion. "These hands, Felicia. They were wrapped around a man's neck with the intent to squeeze the life out of him."

Her tears fell like fat raindrops. "What are you trying to do to me, Spence?"

His heart nearly broke at the sadness in her voice, but he had to go on. Had to know the truth of what she could forgive. He waved his hands under her nose. "Can you look at them, at me, without seeing a monster? Without remembering I almost killed a man?"

She stared at him with agony glimmering in her orbs. Then she shook her head, grabbed her cane and rushed as fast as her disability would allow down the aisle and out of the church.

The door slammed with the combination of her force and the wind whipping.

Spencer sunk to his knees at the altar, staring up at the cross.

Father, forgive me.

"Home. Take me home." Felicia slammed the back door and swiped at her tears.

Blessedly, the driver didn't question her order. She didn't think she could've kept any sort of composure had he asked her anything. She sniffed, fighting to gain control.

Why, God? Why let me feel something for him and then drop this bombshell on me? Oh, sweet Jesus, I can't handle this. I abhor violence.

Her heart ached. Physically. Torturously.

Her tenuous hold on her control threatened to shatter. She clenched and unclenched her fists and willed her stomach to stop roiling, at least until she got home and could be sick in private. Confusion and conflict warred for control of her mind.

The winding dirt roads of the bayou tossed her about in the back seat, causing her nausea to attack in waves. She rolled down the window and drank in the cool air carrying a hint of fish. Within minutes, the driver pulled into the parking lot of her

150

apartment. He appeared at the door, holding out his hand to assist her. "Ms. Felicia, let me walk you to the door. You don't look so good."

Too distraught to argue, she let him lead her around the corner and down the sidewalk. Sick. She was going to be sick.

He jerked her to a stop outside her apartment.

She stared at her door. Standing ajar.

He stepped in front of her. "Call the police from your cell. I'll check things out inside."

Same hymn, different verse. She grabbed his elbow. "No. We'll wait at the car and call the police."

He nodded and followed her back to the parking lot. She called 911, informed Missy of the situation, then closed her phone and stared at the driver whispering into his own cell. "Who're you talking to?"

He snapped his phone closed and feigned innocence. "Are the police on their way?"

"Dispatch is sending Sheriff Theriot. Stop avoiding my question. Who were you talking to?"

The look in his eyes confirmed her suspicions. "You called Luc, yes?"

He didn't answer, but nodded.

Great. Now Luc would rush over and jump feet-first into the investigation. She let out a sigh, not bothering to give the driver a piece of her mind. What was the use? No one ever bothered to listen. Everyone thought her a simpleton. At least that's how they treated her. With kid gloves.

Like a cripple.

Indignation straightened her spine. The nerve of everyone. It was high time she took charge of her circumstances again. With work. Jolie's murder. Kipp Landry. Luc.

And especially with Spencer Bertrand. Her throat closed. Well, once she figured out how she felt about his revelation. She'd sort through that emotional mess later.

A siren wailed in the distance. Then drew closer and closer until the police cruiser spun gravel into the lot. Sheriff Theriot stepped from behind the wheel and ambled toward her. "What's going on, Felicia?"

Funny how she'd never noticed the soft lines around his eyes. Gentleness webs, her grandmother used to call them. Felicia gave herself a mental shake and focused. "My apartment door is open."

"Did you go inside?" The sheriff took steps toward the sidewalk.

"No. We saw the door ajar, came out here and called it in."

He spared her a quick glance. "Sure you shut it when you left?"

Cooyon! "Of course, I'm sure. I've been double-checking ever since . . . since someone killed Jolie."

They rounded the corner. He motioned for her to stay and withdrew his weapon. "Looks like it's been forced open." Gun aimed, he eased to her door and, with his toe, inched it open. Then he disappeared into her apartment.

Felicia held her breath and realized her driver behind her did the same. The corners of her mouth crept up. Seconds fell off the clock. Finally, the sheriff stuck his head out of the doorway. "It's clear, but you need to come see, Felicia."

Dread dogging her every step, she leaned heavily on her cane as she made her way inside her apartment.

As before, the place was in complete disarray. But this time it wasn't ransacked as if someone was searching for something. No, this was a deliberate trashing of the place. Furniture overturned. Picture frames smashed. Pillows and cushions slashed, the stuffing tossed all over the floor.

Destruction.

Felicia's heart pounded. Who would do such a thing? She faced the sheriff. "Kipp?"

"First thing I thought of. Radioed the deputy tailing him. Kipp's been at his place since we released him."

Then who? Her mind raced. She didn't have any enemies. Not that she knew of, anyway.

"You'll want to see this." Sheriff Theriot nodded down the hall to her bedroom.

She gasped as she took it all in. Her comforter lay in shreds. The mattress was sliced to pieces. Even the drapes had been cut. Felicia's heart caught in her throat. "I just can't imagine who'd do suc—"

"Look at the bathroom mirror."

As she stepped into the master bath, her heart skipped a beat. Written in lipstick on the mirror were the words *You're Next.* Her mouth went as dry as Louisiana in August. She caught the sheriff's expression in the mirror.

"Any ideas?" he asked in a mere whisper.

She shook her head and didn't know whether to collapse or be sick. Too much. This was all just too much.

"Whoa. Easy there." Bubba's gentle hand steadied her as he walked her to the bed. Well, to what was left of it. She sank onto the box springs, careful to avoid the deep gashes which would have her falling through to the floor. "I'll get you a glass of water."

He ambled down the hall while Felicia rubbed her arms. The goose bumps wouldn't disappear. She let her gaze drift over her dresser, now void of drawers. They were sprawled over the floor, some in splinters. Someone had to hate her with a vengeance to destroy so much.

Bubba returned with a glass of tap water. She took it with trembling hands and forced down a sip. The water boiled in her stomach.

"I know you're upset, but I need to ask you a few questions."

Felicia stared around the room again, but this time anger shook her hands. "Yes, I'm upset. Someone came into *my* house to destroy it. Threatened *me*."

His eyes widened for a moment, then he pulled the notebook from his front pocket. "Any thoughts on who might have a grievance against you?"

"I can't think of anyone. Except Kipp." She tilted her head. "Is your deputy positive Kipp hasn't left?"

"He's sure."

"Hmm." She took another sip of water. Not that she was thirsty, but it gave her time to think. Who else? Who'd do such a thing? She stood and set the glass on the vanity table. "What about the loan sharks? Maybe Kipp called them and told them I had cash." She gestured about the room. "Maybe this is a threat so I'll give them money."

"Could be. We'll keep checking into their identities." He stared over the room. "But this looks more like something personal, Felicia. Anybody you've upset lately?"

"I don't upset people." But she frowned. "The words . . . they link this to Jolie's murder, yes?"

He nodded. "Unless it's a prankster."

"I don't think so."

"I don't, either. This is too exhaustive." He paused, holding his pencil over the notebook. "Have you upset Pastor Bertrand?"

"What?"

"Well, he does have a past. And he's connected to both you and Jolie."

"Don't we all have a past, Sheriff Theriot?" Why was her indignation rearing its ugly head? The sheriff was right — Spence did have a past. But he'd no more do this to her than she'd try a hula hoop. Of *that,* she was certain. "That's a ridiculous idea, Sheriff."

"I have to check every angle, Felicia."

Not waiting for another question or comment, Felicia stalked down the hallway. Her gait was more pronounced. Her legs ached. It'd been a long day, and she'd about taken all she could. She'd experienced the full gamut of emotions, and her body was just plain worn out.

The front door shoved open just as she entered the living room. Luc filled the doorway, his eyes seeking her. With his scrunched brows, chiseled chin and tensed jaw, he looked anything but happy.

Every ounce of control she had left dissipated like fog over the bayou. He took strides to reach her, holding out his arms. She crumbled into his embrace and let her brother's strength hold her up.

"It's okay. You're safe. I'm taking you home."

Had she the energy, she'd have argued the point. But right then, all she felt was secure.

TWELVE

How had she allowed herself to be so weak when she needed her backbone so badly? Felicia sat at the kitchen table in the Trahan homestead. The notes from Luc's sax drifted down the stairs. His playing usually brought her comfort, but not today. No, today she was mad at herself for allowing her brother to pack her up and bring her home.

"Hello?" CoCo stuck her head in the kitchen door.

Despite her irritation, Felicia smiled. "C'mon in, girl."

Her brother's fiancée gave her a quick hug. "Heard you had a rough time yesterday. I'm so sorry."

CoCo didn't know the half of it. Felicia mustered another smile. "It's okay."

"The sheriff pulled in the driveway behind me."

"Lovely." Felicia rose and poured herself another cup of strong chicory coffee. The aroma filled the kitchen. "Want a cup?"

"Sure."

A loud knock sounded.

"I'll get it," Luc hollered as he bolted down the stairs, saxophone still in hand.

Felicia rolled her eyes and handed CoCo a mug of steaming java. Both sat at the table as Luc and the sheriff wandered into the kitchen.

"CoCo, Felicia." The sheriff nodded in their direction.

"Let me get you a cup of coffee, Bubba. Just have a seat." Luc made his way to the coffeepot.

"We ran some tests on your apartment last night," the sheriff told Felicia. "We have the statistical report back on what kind of knife was used to slice up your place."

Great. Knives and sickos, the breakfast of champions. Felicia waited.

"According to the preliminary reports, the knife used at your apartment is the same style as the one used to murder Jolie."

Did that mean it was the same person? The killer, come back to take her out? Felicia tensed her shoulders to ward off the shiver.

"We're working every angle that connects you and Jolie."

"She was my best friend. We lived together, worked at the same place, went to the same church — *your* church, too . . . there are connections everywhere."

"And we're checking all of them." Bubba accepted the cup from Luc, took a sip and stared into Felicia's eyes. "We'll stay on top of this until we get a break. In the meantime, I think it's smart for you to stay here."

Luc laid his hand on Felicia's shoulder. It was her undoing.

"I appreciate your concern, Sheriff, but I need to get back to my home and put things in order."

"No." Luc said but a single word, yet it was adamant.

Felicia stood and faced her brother. "Yes. I need to call my insurance company, take pictures and such." She glanced at the sheriff. "Are you finished gathering whatever evidence you need?"

His eyes met Luc's for a second. "Well, uh, technically . . ."

"Then I can start my process, yes?"

"*Boo,* I think you should let me take care of it." Luc tightened his grip on her shoulder.

"It's nice of you, but I can handle this myself. It's my home, my things, my *life* that's been plundered. I can take care of it."

The sheriff shifted his weight uncomfortably. "I've got to get going." He set his cup on the counter. "I'll see y'all later."

The kitchen screen door shut with a slam.

"We know you *can* handle this yourself, but why don't you let Luc do it?" CoCo's eyes were soft and gentle.

Felicia shrugged out of Luc's hold. "Look, I appreciate what y'all are trying to do, I really do, but I have to do this." She faced her brother. "I'm a grown woman and would've been married by now had . . . had circumstances been different. I'm quite capable of handling this situation."

"But you shouldn't have to. Besides, I want you to stay here where I know you're safe." Luc smiled.

"I know you do. But I can't keep running back here every time something happens."

"Why not? This is your home."

She gave a soft smile and touched her brother's hand. "No, Luc, it isn't. Not anymore." She ran a hand over her hair. "I need you to understand this. I love living at my apartment and doing things by myself. Even grocery shopping is a blessing because it's *me* buying food for *me*."

"You can do the grocery shopping here."

Felicia shook her head. "You don't get it. I have to take charge of my life. For years, I sat on the sidelines and didn't take part in the game of life. I sat in that stupid wheel-chair for way too many years, all because Grandfather didn't want me to try a new medical procedure." She held up her hand when Luc opened his mouth.

"I didn't marry Frank as soon as he asked because he was a suspect in Grandfather's murder. I should've trusted my own heart, but he wanted to wait until he'd officially been cleared. By that time, it was too late."

"Fel—"

"No, Luc, I need you to listen. To grasp what I'm trying to tell you." She flipped her hair over her shoulder. "I stayed here longer than I should have after my surgery because it was easier to let you and Mom take care of me. You didn't want me to have to worry about falling or getting hurt. And while that's sweet of you, and I know you only act like this because you love me, it's not what's best for me."

"I'm only trying to help you."

"I know that. But life's about falling and getting hurt. I can't be sheltered my entire life, Luc. I've let the men in my life control my actions since before I can remember. Grandfather, Frank, you —"

"I don't control you." Luc's eyes hardened.

"Listen to her." CoCo stood and grabbed

162

Luc's hand. "She's right. You need to understand how she feels."

Felicia smiled at her friend. "I'm not saying you do anything with bad intentions. It's just that I have to make my own choices, my own decisions. Right or wrong, they're mine to make. Fail or succeed, I want it to be *my* doing."

"But I'm your big brother. I'm supposed to watch out for you."

She laid a hand on his arm. "You do, and I love you for it. But you have to let me live my own life. Whether you like it or not, I have to do things on my own. Try to understand."

Long seconds hung in the air as murky as swamp water. Finally, Luc pulled her into a tight hug. "I understand. I'll try to keep quiet. No promises, but I'll do my best."

Felicia eased back and smiled. "That's all I can ask, yes?"

The cleanup process went much quicker than Felicia could've ever hoped. CoCo and Tara had come with her to the apartment, sleeves rolled up and ready to work. Four hours later, the living room and kitchen were put back to order. Well, as much as they could be. The trash had been bagged and salvageable furniture righted. They

163

might not look as nice as they had before, but at least it looked like *her* home again. The list of items to be replaced had run over to a second page. Good thing she didn't have to worry about money on top of everything else since her family was well-off.

"Mark's on the phone." Tara held out the cordless they'd found buried under the upturned garbage can.

Oh, no. She'd forgotten to call and cancel her physical therapy this morning. She lodged the phone against her shoulder and cheek. "Hey, Mark. I'm so sorry."

"Standing me up, are ya?"

"I had a break-in at my place again last night."

"Heard about that. I was really just calling to check on you."

"That's sweet." She paused as his words sank in. "Wait a minute. How'd you hear about it?"

"Sheriff came by, questioning everyone you work with down here."

Now, that was barking up the wrong tree.

"So, are you okay?"

"I'm fine."

"I'll take you at your word. We still on for tomorrow morning?"

"Nine o'clock sharp. I'll be there. I'm

really sorry about flaking out today."

"You're entitled. I'll just work you double hard tomorrow."

She groaned, then laughed. "Thanks, Mark." She tossed the phone onto the couch missing two of the three cushions. Something else she'd have to order.

Couch cushions. The Queen Anne wasn't salvageable and had to be thrown out. Ninety percent of her dishes. Mattress. Curtains. Pillows. All had to be replaced. The enormity of it all staggered her. She dropped to the single couch cushion.

"Hey, we'll get it done. Stop looking defeated." Tara propped her hands on her hips, glaring.

Just what she needed — a kick in the behind. Felicia giggled and mustered to her feet. "Right. I'm going to take another load to the Dumpster."

Tara nodded. "Good. I'm going to tackle the bathroom."

Smiling to herself, Felicia grabbed two trash bags and dragged them out the door. She lifted one and trekked down the side-walk. Soon though, her legs protested with cramps and spasms. Felicia dropped the bag and leaned against a support pole.

A young woman, one Felicia had seen around the complex lately, wandered down the walkway. "Need some help?"

Her voice was familiar. Had she talked to Felicia before? Maybe in the laundry room? Felicia couldn't remember. "No, thanks. I'm just a little sore."

"Didn't you used to be in a wheelchair?"

"Yes. I'm up to walking with a cane now."

"Well, congratulations. See ya." The young woman rushed down the walk and turned the corner to the parking lot.

Felicia stared after her for a long minute. Something wasn't right. She couldn't put her finger on what was amiss, but something about the woman definitely rang bells in Felicia's head.

But why?

Miracle upon miracles, not a single employee quit, running from the center in disgust or fear.

Spencer dismissed the meeting with his operators. None condemned him for his past. Amazingly, they seemed to understand and accept. They'd exhibited nothing but grace. Grace that could only have been extended through God. He stared heavenward and mouthed *thank you.*

Had he misjudged his congregation and the citizens of Lagniappe, as well?

Felicia?

He'd pushed her hard last night. Been too aggressive. Got in her face. Hurt her. The tears weren't just for show, not with Felicia.

Shame and regret had tormented him all night. His sleep had been fitful at best, nightmarish at worst. He owed her an apology. Then he'd leave her alone. He'd broken his own boundary where she was concerned, and now she'd been hurt. It was all his fault.

It must be his cross to bear — the women he cared about were destined to be hurt. Carrie. Mom. Felicia.

Michael's voice vibrated over the intercom. "Felicia on line two for you, boss."

Unnerving. He snatched up the receiver. "Hello, Felicia."

"Uh, hi." Her voice came out breathy, as if she'd been lifting weights. "I'm just calling to let you know I won't be in tonight."

"Are you okay? Everything all right?"

"I'm fine. I just need a break."

From work, or him? "I see. No problem. You have plenty of personal days you haven't used."

"Yeah." She hesitated. He didn't know whether to say anything else or not. She deserved his apology in person, not on the phone. Her sigh filled the connection. "Look, I might as well give you a heads-up.

My apartment was broken into again last night."

His heart stalled. "Kipp?"

"No. He was under surveillance. Anyway, the sheriff is making rounds and questioning everybody I know. Just wanted to let you know he'd probably show up at the center to ask questions, if he hasn't already."

"Are you okay?"

"I'm fine. Cleaning up."

"Do you need any help?" He ran a hand over his face. As if she'd want help from him after last night.

"CoCo and Tara are helping. Luc'll be by after he gets off work to carry away the stuff we can't save."

"Is it bad?"

"It'll be all right. Gotta go, just wanted to let you know not to expect me at work. Bye."

She hung up before he had a chance to say anything else. Guess that told him a lot. She didn't want his help. Didn't want to see him. Didn't really sound like she wanted to even talk to him.

What did he expect? He'd known she was too good for him — had tried to keep his distance from her in the months she'd worked for him. Yet, he hadn't been able to stop falling in love with her.

He brought himself up, taking stock of his

emotions.

Oh, no. He *was* in love with her.

And there wasn't a thing he could do to make things right with her. Not now.

Except pray.

THIRTEEN

"Wesley Ellender's been arrested for the murder of Jolie Landry."

Felicia stared at the television. Wes? Charged with Jolie's murder? No way. She turned up the volume on the remote and inched to the edge of her seat.

Sheriff Theriot fielded questions from the media on the steps of the courthouse. Reporters flocked around him like ants at a picnic. Microphones grappled for better placement. "We recovered the murder weapon from Mr. Ellender's possession," he announced.

Felicia gasped and sank back against the new chair Luc had delivered earlier. Wes had the murder weapon? No, it couldn't be. She couldn't have been that wrong about him! If so, she'd all but pushed Jolie into the arms of her killer. Guilt dropped over her and settled between her shoulder blades.

The television cut to a commercial.

Why hadn't Sheriff Theriot called her? She hated being excluded from the case.

She rose to her feet and on shaky legs went to the kitchen. Grabbing a bottle of water from the refrigerator, she sucked in a big gulp right as the phone rang, startling her. She flinched and leaked the last remaining bit of water onto the counter before grabbing the phone and tossing a towel over the spill. "Hello."

"Why didn't you tell me there was a threat left in your apartment?" Spence sounded more angry than annoyed.

"It wasn't important. Have you seen the news?"

"Of course it's important. Felicia, someone directly threatened you."

"Who told you, anyway?"

"The sheriff. Why didn't *you* tell me?"

"It was implied. Nothing major. Have you seen the news?"

"Not this afternoon. Why?"

"They've arrested Wes."

"Jolie's boyfriend?"

"Yes. I can't believe this."

"They must be pretty sure he's guilty if they arrested him, Felicia."

She bit her tongue against the sharp retort burning there. "They say they found the murder weapon in his possession."

He sucked in air. "I'm coming over."

"No, I don—" But he'd already hung up.

Felicia rushed to her bathroom, one of the two rooms still in disarray. She stared at herself in the bathroom mirror, startled at what she saw. Yes, her hair was a mess and her face smudged from all the cleaning she'd done, but it was the words that drew her attention.

The words that Tara had scrubbed off the mirror. Yet, Felicia could still see them.

Had Wes destroyed her apartment and left her such a message?

Her reflection blinked back at her. Wes couldn't have done such a thing. Why, even if he *had* killed Jolie, what would be his motive in coming after Felicia?

It made no sense.

She grabbed a washcloth, saturated it with cool water, and scrubbed her face free of the grime and sweat. Once that task was completed, she ran a brush through her hair. Catching her expression in the mirror, Felicia tossed the brush into the basket.

She was flushed, and not from exertion. How could she be excited about Spence coming by at such a time? Or anytime, for that matter. She shouldn't care what she looked like.

But she did.

The doorbell buzzed.

Felicia stuck her tongue out at her mirror image and headed down the hallway. She checked the peephole before she swung open the door. "You didn't have to come over."

Spence ignored her comment and brushed past her into the apartment. He glanced around the room before facing her. "Are you really okay?"

"I'm fine. You wasted a trip."

"Felicia, you exasperate me in ways I never thought possible."

She exasperated *him?* Was he nuts? "Look, I don't know what you hoped to accomp—"

He pulled her into his arms and planted his lips on hers, silencing her protest very effectively. She went rigid at first, but in the space of a heartbeat, she relaxed. Her heart thudded as she wrapped her arms around his neck. He deepened the kiss, and she let go of her confusing emotions.

He stepped back, his breathing shaky. "We need to talk."

Talk? As if she could string together two words to form a coherent thought after that kiss. He *was* nuts.

"I want to apologize. I had no right to be so brusque with you last night."

Brusque would be an interesting term to describe his behavior. She thought rude would be more accurate.

"It's just that I've kept the secret for so long. Trying to keep anyone from uncovering my past and making snap judgments about me like before." He shook his head. "I didn't want everyone to reject me. That was wrong. I should've been upfront and honest. In trying to avoid judgment, I misjudged everyone. I didn't trust them to extend grace."

She fidgeted. His analysis hit a little too close to the truth for her liking.

"I didn't trust *you* enough, and I should have. I'm so sorry."

He really knew how to slam it home. Another layer of guilt settled in her spirit.

The phone rang. She grabbed the cordless from the couch. "Hello?"

"Did you hear about Wesley Ellender?" CoCo sounded breathless.

"Yeah. It's awful."

"But that means you're safe. Luc won't have any reason to try to worm you into moving home."

Felicia laughed. "True."

"What's wrong? You don't sound relieved."

"I don't think Wes killed Jolie, and I sure don't believe he trashed my house and

174

wrote a threat on my bathroom mirror."

"But the police said they found the murder weapon —"

"I know. I think there's been a big mistake."

CoCo hesitated. "Are you sure you just don't want to believe it? I mean, it's hard to deny the evidence of the murder weapon."

"Like when the sheriff discovered Grandfather's gun missing, then found it in the bayou? That's what put Luc at the top of the suspect list in Grandfather's murder."

"True. What're you going to do?"

"Try to figure it out." Determination came over her in a flash. "I'm going to see the sheriff and get some answers."

"Do you want me to come get you?"

Felicia glanced at Spence, who made no pretense of not listening in on her conversation. "No. Spence is here, and I'll ask him to drive me."

He nodded.

"Well, okay. Let me know what you find out."

"Sure." Felicia hung up.

"You really believe Wesley's innocent?"

She faced Spence. "I do. I can't believe he'd kill Jolie. He loved her. Well, he was falling in love with her."

"How do you know?"

"Know what?"

"That he was falling in love with her?"

She shrugged. "I don't know. I just sensed that when I was around the two of them."

"You normally sense things like that?"

"Yes. No. I don't know." Why did he ask such questions? And why had he kissed her? No, she wouldn't open up that topic of discussion. Not yet. Not until she could analyze her own emotions. "Will you drive me to the sheriff's office now?"

The pronouncement of his love for her lingered in Spencer's mouth. He knew he had to clamp it down. He couldn't tell her how he felt. Not now. Too much distracted her. Eventually, she'd be able to get beyond his past, his lies, his secrets. Maybe by the grace of God, she'd be able to someday understand. Just not yet.

But she'd responded to his kiss. That filled him with hope.

He studied Felicia as they waited to see the sheriff. Her soft hair hung like a halo around her face, drawing out her stunning eyes. What a stark comparison to the ugliness of the police station. She was a vision, made more so by the light in her eyes reflecting the gentleness of her soul. A gentleness nearly destroyed by life. She'd certainly had her fair share of rough knocks, yet she kept going, showing her strong resolve.

He admired her all the more.

"Felicia. Pastor." The sheriff stood at the counter. "How can I help you?"

She rose. "I'd like to talk to you about Jolie's case."

Sheriff Theriot ran a hand over his red hair. "Surely you've heard we've made an arrest. Wesley Ellender."

Spencer moved behind Felicia as she stepped closer and lowered her voice. "You found the knife?"

He nodded. "In his car. The blood on it matches Jolie's. And we found a fiber matching your curtains on it as well. Lab verified the results this morning — we had them rush to get them back." The sheriff smiled. "Open-and-shut case. You can rest easy now."

She held the edge of the counter. "Are you sure?"

"Yes." He let a minute slip by, wariness etching into the lines around his eyes. "Do you doubt it?"

"I just don't see his motive for trashing my place."

He laughed. "Who knows why people snap and do what they do?" The sheriff's gaze drifted to Spencer.

Spencer's heartbeat kicked into overdrive, but he bit his tongue to keep from responding. He'd better get used to the slams and innuendos. More would surely come.

Felicia tapped her nail on the Formica counter. "It's not logical. Why leave me the message? I wasn't a threat to him."

"We'll cover that in the interrogation. We have to wait for his lawyer to get here to question him."

"What about the loan sharks?"

"We're beginning to believe the loan shark story was a lie Kipp told his sister to try to get money from her. No one has come forward to collect on any debt that we've been able to determine since Kipp's release." The sheriff shrugged. "Even word on the street is that Kipp Landry needed money to go gamble. No one would give him a line of credit. Since his release, he hasn't left his place."

"Doesn't that strike you as odd?" She recalled the look in his eyes. "He was so desperate."

"Who knows? I'm just assured the man hasn't left his residence since being released."

The sheriff laid his hand over hers. "Felicia, I know you don't want to believe Wesley's her killer, but all the evidence points directly to him." He patted her hand. "Why don't you go on home and let the matter drop? You can find out all the details at Wesley's trial."

What a dismissal. Nice, but a dismissal, nonetheless. Spencer waited for her reaction.

She let out a sigh. "I still think you're wrong, Sheriff."

"I can't deny the evidence."

Felicia and the sheriff exchanged long stares, then she nodded. She turned to face Spencer. "Take me home now?"

She remained silent on the walk to his truck and the entire drive back to her apartment. When he parked, she got out before he could make it around the vehicle to open her door. He trailed two steps behind her.

"Felicia, wait."

"What?"

"I think we need to finish our talk."

"I'm exhausted. Can't it wait?"

He didn't want to put this off any longer. He wanted her to tell him how she felt. Yell at him, smack him in the chest, throw something at his head . . . any kind of reaction. As he studied her, he noticed the dark circles under her eyes. Her skin didn't look as bright as normal, either.

179

He rolled his fingers into his palm and fought to make his voice even. "Sure. You'll be at work tomorrow?"

"Planning on it." She opened her door. "Good night, Spence."

The door closed in his face, slamming his heart to the ground. It was no less than he deserved.

He plodded to the parking lot, lost in the cruelty of his situation. He nearly tripped over his own steps as he swerved to avoid hitting a woman cutting across the sidewalk. Man, he sure was preoccupied. He'd better get his head on straight before he tried to drive back to the center.

He sat in his truck, praying for direction. A car peeled out of the lot, shooting loose gravel against his truck. He jerked his head. Where was that woman going in such a hurry?

Spencer let out a sigh and turned over the engine.

Sometimes, life just seemed too much to deal with.

FOURTEEN

The spicy aroma of the boudin sausage in the jambalaya permeated the Trahan kitchen. Felicia's stomach rumbled.

"How does the table look?"

Felicia smiled at CoCo, who hadn't changed out of her church dress before she'd rushed over to help prepare lunch. "Lovely. It's nice of you to come help celebrate Mom's homecoming."

"She'll be my mother-in-law soon. I should be here."

"I'm sorry about that. Getting her for an in-law, I mean."

CoCo grabbed glasses and filled them with ice. "Hattie's okay. Besides, you have to take the good with the bad."

The good with the bad? An image of Spence's face filled her vision. Had she only been willing to accept the good with him? Would she allow the bad to outweigh the good? She stiffened as she stirred the thick rice mixture. Was she so shallow?

A horn sounded from the driveway.

"They're here." CoCo fingered her long curls. "Do I look all right?"

How cute for her to be so nervous about Hattie Trahan's opinion. Felicia grinned. "You're beautiful."

CoCo gave a snort and playfully slapped at Felicia's arm. "Yeah. Sure. Right." She turned and opened the front door.

Her brother's fiancée moved with such grace. Such natural flowing movements. Felicia blinked back hot tears. Would she ever lose the cane and walk alone, much less with such poise?

"Oh, my. It's downright sticky outside." Hattie dropped into a chair at the table. She narrowed her eyes at Felicia. "Nice of you to make it."

Felicia swallowed. Her mother obviously hadn't had a personality change in rehab. "It's nice to see you, too, Mom. I made your favorite."

"Here, let me get you some iced tea." CoCo poured a glass.

After taking a sip, Hattie fanned herself with the cloth napkin and continued to scrutinize Felicia. "So, Luc tells me you're staying in that apartment of yours."

Starting already. Felicia wadded the dish

towel in her hand. "Yes, I am."

"Heard on the news they arrested that Wesley character for the murder."

"Yes." Felicia gritted her teeth.

"I'd never trust an Ellender. Why, Mr. Ellender Senior — that'd be Wesley's grandfather — he was always up to no good. I remember about a year ago, he hi—"

"Mom, why don't we eat? My stomach's grumbling, and the food smells divine." Luc plopped down beside her.

She laid a hand on his cheek and let out a titter. "My boy. Always hungry." She raked her gaze over CoCo. "You a good cook? My Luc's got a manly appetite."

"Oh, yes, ma'am. I love to cook."

"But *can* you?"

Her mother would never quit. Felicia set the serving bowl of steaming jambalaya in the center of the table. "Let's eat before it gets cold."

"Oh, well, yes. We can't have lunch cold." Hattie reached for the serving spoon.

"Would you like me to say grace, Mom?" Luc's eyes twinkled with mischief.

"Oh. Of course." Their mother folded her hands politely in her lap. She might have her faults, but lacking gentility wasn't one of them.

Felicia caught Luc's wink before she

ducked her head. She barely heard her brother's blessing as she sent up her own silent prayer.

Please, God, show me what to do about Spence. Help me to follow Your leading, because I'm totally confused.

Felicia made her way into the sheriff's office, which housed the jail in the basement. She didn't know the proper protocol to see someone in the parish lockup, but desperation made her determined.

The sheriff's dispatcher, Missy, met her at the counter. "Why, Felicia Trahan, what brings you down here on a Sunday afternoon?"

"I'd like to visit Wesley Ellender."

"Whatever for, hon?"

Felicia licked her lips. "It's personal."

Missy raised one of her finely tweezed brows. "Hmm. Does the sheriff know about this visit?"

"I didn't realize I needed the sheriff's permission to visit an old friend." Felicia squared her shoulders. "So, do I need to fill out any paperwork or anything to visit Mr. Ellender?"

"Hang on a minute." Missy sashayed across the room, disappearing in the back.

Felicia let out a pent-up breath and tapped

her fingernail against the counter.

"Hear you wanna see Wesley," boomed a voice from the opposite side of the room.

Felicia pushed her gaze to Deputy Gary Anderson. Well, she'd probably fare better facing the burly deputy rather than the sheriff. "I do." Wow, her voice didn't even crack. Nancy Drew, look out!

Anderson ambled to the counter. "What about?"

"It's personal." She met his stare dead-on.

"Want me to try the sheriff?" Missy asked, lifting a phone.

Felicia glared.

"Nah. Sunday's a regular visitin' day." He shrugged. "Sheriff didn't say Wesley couldn't have any visitors."

"Are you sure you don't want me to check?" Missy clutched the telephone.

"Don't bother him."

The phone clattered back onto its cradle. Felicia smiled at Anderson as he opened the swinging door and nodded toward the hallway. "Follow me."

Right inside the doorway, the hall gave a sharp left. Another left, and they stood before an elevator. Deputy Anderson inserted a key and the light over the door lit. "Security," he said.

The walls closed in on them. Felicia struggled to breathe normally as they stepped into the service elevator. It was very small. Very confined. With another twist of Anderson's key, the doors slid closed and they jerked downward.

On the positive side, there was something to be said for an elevator, however archaic. At least she didn't have to mess with stairs.

The car jolted to a stop, and her heart leapt into her throat. Deputy Anderson grinned. "It's a little rusty. We don't get many people in the holding cells, normally. Maybe a kid or two being held to sleep off the aftereffects of a party."

The doors slid open, and he motioned her to exit first. Good thing — she itched to claw her way into more breathing space.

They followed a short corridor, stopping at a barred door blocking the hall. Anderson unlocked it, swinging it open with a squeak. She passed through the iron doorway, fighting off a shiver.

He stopped her at the first door on the right, slipping his key into the lock. "This is the visiting room. You can sit at one of the tables. I'll bring Wesley in from another door." He scratched at the stubble on his chin. "We've never had someone in for a violent crime have a visitor."

"Is that a problem?"

"Well. . . ." More chin rubbing. "We don't have a separator."

"I'm not concerned."

"But policy states —"

"You just said you've never had a visitor for someone being held for a violent crime. That means there is no policy." She crossed her arms over her chest.

He hesitated, as if weighing the options. "I guess it'll be all right. I'll stand right outside the door. If you need help, you just holler."

She nodded. Need help? No, she refused to believe Wesley was violent. She stepped into the room and took a seat at one of the two picnic-style tables. She gripped the handle of her cane. A fine coat of sweat lined her palm.

The other door to the room opened with a creak. They really needed to oil every hinge in the building. Wesley entered, handcuffs holding his hands in front of his body. With a hand on Wesley's shoulder, Deputy Anderson led him to the opposite side of the table from Felicia. "You sit here and don't move. I'll be right outside."

When they were alone, Wesley lifted his glazed stare to her. "I didn't do it, Felicia."

"I know. That's why I'm here."

"What am I gonna do?"

"Tell me about the knife they found."

"I don't know how it got in my car. I never saw it before in my life."

She licked her lips and glanced at the door. She could make out Anderson's silhouette in the little window of the adjoining door. "Tell me what happened."

"I've been in and out of my car since the night Jolie was murdered. You know this. I met you at your apartment in my car."

A chilling reminder that he did have means and opportunity. And motive, if the sheriff was correct. But would he have had time? Jolie had been stabbed multiple times. Blood had been all over the apartment. Felicia swallowed back the bile. Would Wes have had time to change before meeting her at the apartment to find Jolie? Did the police know something she didn't?

"When I left that night after the police finished questioning me, a deputy walked me to my car. Like even if I'd done such a horrible thing, I'd just slip the knife under the driver's seat? I'm not that stupid."

Or, had he done it for this reason alone — to use as an argument?

"I've driven that car several times over, at least twice a day, since she died. That knife wasn't in there."

He could be lying.

"And then the police said there were fibers on it from some vandalism at your apartment." He stared straight into her eyes. "I didn't do that, Felicia. I promise, I didn't." He didn't blink, didn't break eye contact.

And she knew. He was telling the truth.

"When did they find the knife?"

"Yesterday morning. Early. They showed up at my house around seven-thirty. I was still in bed when they pounded on the door."

"Did they have a warrant?"

He nodded. "I'd already retained that Dwayne Williams you recommended. I called him and he came over. Said it was a duly-served warrant to check my home and my car."

The sheriff must've had a strong lead about the murder weapon to get a judge to sign a warrant on a Saturday. Hmm, she'd have to ask him about that when she got the chance. "Which did they check first?"

"My car."

Sounded like someone tipped off the police. "Do you keep your car locked?"

He hung his head. "I never saw the need." He lifted his head and gave a casual shrug. "We live in Lagniappe. Who'd think someone would break into a car here?"

He had a point. Then again, in the past

year, Lagniappe sure seemed to be on a crime roll. It was downright disheartening.

"I was shocked when they pulled the knife out. They held it up and asked me if it was one of mine. I assured them it wasn't." He rubbed absently at the handcuffs around his wrists. "They bagged it and searched the house, paying close attention to the kitchen. They couldn't find a matching one."

"What kind of knife is it?"

"One that fits in those butcher-block things. I didn't really get to examine it closely before I was arrested."

From a set. "They didn't take anything from the house?"

"The clothes I was wearing the night Jolie was killed. Even though I'd washed them since then."

Deputy Anderson strode into the room. "Time's up." He grabbed Wesley's elbow and tugged him to his feet.

"I'm innocent, Felicia."

She believed him. "Stay strong. I'll be praying for you."

"I'll be back to get you in a minute," Deputy Anderson said.

Within minutes of Wesley disappearing, Anderson returned to the other door. "*Allons.* I'll take you back up."

The elevator wasn't as creepy as she

remembered. "Deputy, can I ask you something? Since Wesley's in jail and all."

"Sure." He puffed his chest out a little. Maybe he was tired of being in Bubba's shadow. She could use that.

"Isn't it difficult to get in touch with a judge on a weekend? Especially during Mardi Gras season?"

"Sure is. I had to run over to the other side of the parish to get it signed and get back. All before the judge left for his golf match."

That explained the early hour. "Which judge?"

"Leo Holtz."

Felicia blinked as the elevator door opened. Judge Holtz wasn't a hanging judge. He had the reputation of being fair and just. Someone who wouldn't be bothered signing a warrant on his golf day without very good reason.

They turned down the last leg of the corridor. Now or never.

She smiled sweetly and touched Anderson's arm. "You must be very important for the sheriff to trust you with something so vital."

His chest stuck out a little farther. "Well, we had that anonymous tip about the murder weapon being in Wesley's car. Bubba called the judge and caught him just in time. Holtz was worried we'd make him miss his tee time, but I raced all the way there."

"Yeah. That knife. What kind was it again?"

"One of those fancy-smancey handled numbers that you get over at Miller's."

The one ritzy store in town. Interesting.

Smiling, she opened the door to the station. "Thanks so much." She couldn't resist giving a finger wave to Missy on her way out.

So, someone had called in a tip about the knife. In Felicia's opinion, it was an obvious plant. Only the murderer could have planted the knife because the police hadn't found it on the site or discarded.

But who had planted it?

FIFTEEN

What now?

Spencer froze as Sheriff Theriot made his way across the center to the office. The operators followed him with their gaze. Probably expecting another revelation into Spencer's past. He couldn't blame them. Not really. Felicia stood, her stare never leaving the sheriff's movements.

The sheriff rapped on the door. "Pastor?"

"Come on in, Sheriff." Spencer waved at the chair in front of his desk.

The lawman shook his head. "I won't be here that long. Just came by to tell you we've officially closed our investigation into the center." He paused. "And you."

Spencer let out the breath he hadn't realized he'd been holding. "Oh. Good."

"And I wanted to apologize for just blurting out your past in front of your staff. That was rude of me."

Rude? Hardly. Humiliating, yes.

"That's okay."

"No, it's not. I followed up with Jon Garrison this morning."

Spencer tried not to fidget. "And?"

"He speaks highly of you. For a Yankee and all." Sheriff Theriot smiled.

Spencer grinned. "Yeah. It was a little difficult to understand him when I first started reporting to him. I've gotten used to it now."

The sheriff glanced around, pink darkening his cheeks. "So, are we good?" He extended his hand.

Spencer accepted the olive branch. "We're good."

Sheriff Theriot gave a half cough. "Guess I'd better be on my way, then. Just wanted to come by and tell you in person."

"I appreciate that." It took a big man to make the gesture the sheriff had made.

Felicia barged into his office. "What's going on?"

Despite his heart aching just at the sight of her, Spencer smiled. "Nothing. Sheriff Theriot just wanted to tell me they've closed the investigation into the center."

"Oh." She seemed flustered, her fingers tapping the handle of her cane. "That's good."

The sheriff nodded. "Now that we have the murder weapon and the suspect behind bars, y'all can start putting your lives back together. Get some closure."

Felicia licked her lips. Not necessarily a good sign. Sometimes that meant she was about to step out on a boat with no life jacket. "I heard the knife came from a set you can order over at Miller's. A little unusual, don't you think, Sheriff, that a bachelor would have such a set?"

Sheriff Theriot's brows crunched into a single line. "How do you know what kind of knife it was?"

"And did you check it for fingerprints?"

"The handle was wiped clean, as we expected. Probably wore gloves." He shook his head. "Felicia Trahan, I told you to stay out of this investigation."

"Just wondering." She lifted a single shoulder. "Seemed a little odd to me."

The sheriff pointed at her, his eyes narrowing behind his glasses. "You keep your nose out of this. We're following up on the knives, and everything else on the case."

She turned and fingered a sheet of paper on the edge of Spencer's desk. A good man would try to ease her discomfort. The time had come for him to be that man. "Thanks again for coming by, Sheriff. I really appreciate it."

Sheriff Theriot nodded, cast a final glare

at Felicia and ambled out of the office.

"Want to tell me what's with all the questions?" Spencer leaned against his desk. A slight movement, but one that put him in closer proximity to her. If he inhaled deeply, he could even smell the flowery shampoo she used. Is that what he'd been reduced to — stealing whiffs of her perfume, making unnecessary movements just to be closer to her?

A heavy silence hung between them. Felicia glanced to the floor. "I've been mulling over everything and still can't believe Wes killed Jolie. Even the way they knew about the knife reeks of a setup."

"What're you talking about?"

"Uh . . . well, um, I understand they got an anonymous tip about the knife being in Wes's car. That's how they were able to get a warrant. On a Saturday and all." Her cheeks were tinged a flattering shade of pink.

"And you know this how?"

"Deputy Anderson told me."

"When was this?" A funny feeling fluttered in his gut.

"Yesterday."

"Where'd you see Deputy Anderson on Sunday?" The good lawman didn't attend Felicia's church. Anderson was a member of Spencer's congregation.

She finally met his gaze before glancing over her shoulder. "I should get back to my station."

"Felicia, what are you doing?"

A look fell across her face that indicated she wanted to spill her guts and his question had just granted her permission. "Why would Wesley Ellender have such an expensive and fancy knife set? Most bachelors grab anything. Luc would, except he's at home and uses Mom's." She tossed him a questioning look. "What about you? Do you have a nice set of knives?"

He laughed, picturing his utensil drawer. "Mine don't even match."

"Exactly." She tapped a finger against her chin. "I just think the sheriff is too easily satisfied with the notion of Wes being the killer. And he's not. Wes had no reason to trash my place, and I don't think he could've gotten cleaned up quickly enough."

Words froze on his tongue. She was so beautiful, so determined-looking, it nearly broke his heart. "Felicia, can we talk? About you and me?"

Her eyes widened, and she took a step backward. "This isn't the place."

"Can I drive you home, then? We can stop and get a cup of coffee."

"I don't kn—"

"Please?"

"Well . . ."

"Just one cup? Please?" Yeah, he was begging, but he was also beyond caring. Desperate situations called for desperate measures. "You can tell me more about these knives."

"Okay." With that, she left his office and returned to her station.

A cup of coffee. Who'd have thought his heart would race over a date for a single cup of coffee?

The clock's hands moved as fast as a fan's blades on high.

Why had she agreed to let Spence drive her home? And to talk to him over coffee? She must be losing her mind. She had no idea what to say. How to act. She didn't even know what she felt for him.

Another ten minutes fell off the clock.

Calls trickled in, most of them easy to handle. Someone just wanting an ear to listen. Felicia could provide that, even if her mind wasn't on the caller's problems.

More notices of the upcoming Masquerade Mardi Gras Ball hung around the center. Would Spence still want her to go with him? If so, did she still want to?

Fifteen more minutes gone.

Okay, God, I need something. Some direction, some guidance. Soon I'll face Spence. What do You want me to do?

Only the phone ringing sounded.

"Vermilion Parish Community Christian Hotline. This is Felicia."

"Recording me? Gonna turn me over to the police again?"

Felicia's heartbeat pounded in her head. Winnie! She stood and waved at Spence, who stared at her from the window in his office. "Winnie?"

"Yeah. Didn't think you'd hear from me again, did ya?"

"I'm glad you called back."

Spence appeared at her side and silently plugged in another set of headphones.

"Bet you are."

"How are you? Not trying to plot revenge on your ex, are you?"

"As if I'd tell you if I were. You're a snitch."

Felicia pressed her lips tight and glared at Spence. "I'm sorry you feel that way."

"Yeah, well. My ex got his, I made skippy sure of that."

Apprehension stole her breath. "What'd you do, Winnie?"

"Like I'm gonna tell you? Puhleeze." The laugh over the phone was more of a cackle.

"I'm trying to help you."

"Sure you are. You can't even help yourself. Limping around with that cane, riding in that fancy limo of yours with a spiffy driver. Yeah, you're really trying to help little ole me."

Ice settled in the pit of her stomach. Spence grabbed her hand and moved to activate his microphone. Felicia shook her head. "You know who I am?"

A snort followed by laughter. "I've known who you were since the first time you answered the phone. You think you're so high and mighty and above the rest of us, don't ya? Well, all your money didn't stop that quack from breaking into your place, did it?"

"How did you —"

"That's right, princess, you aren't untouchable. I think I've had enough of *your* help. I won't be calling again."

The click echoed over the line. Felicia slammed the receiver back to its cradle while Spence laid down his headset. She stood slowly.

"Felicia?"

She spun and faced him. "Nobody knew about my break-ins. The sheriff gagged the press from even mentioning it, hoping it'd lure Kipp to contact the loan sharks." Fear slithered around her like moss on a tree. "How'd she know?"

"I don't know, but we'll find out." He laid an arm around her shoulders.

Warmth seeped into her bones. "How?"

"We'll figure it out. I'll order a tap on the phones."

"You can't do that. That'd be in violation of what we advertise — no caller ID, no star 69, no traces. Besides, she said she wasn't calling again."

"And she's said that before."

Felicia dropped her gaze to the floor. This Winnie knew too much about her personal business. It left her cold.

Spence hugged her tighter. "We'll figure it out."

She lifted her gaze. "Can I have a rain check for tonight? I don't feel much like coffee or talking. If you don't mind, I'd just as soon have my driver take me on home."

Disappointment crept into his eyes. "Do you think that's a good idea? After Winnie's call and all?"

"She didn't threaten me or anything. And even when she did threaten her ex's girl-friend, she let that go." She moved away from him and glanced at the clock. "I forgot to call my driver to tell him you'd be taking me home, anyway. He should be here by now."

"Let me walk you out, at least."

She didn't have the will to resist. His hand was steady under her elbow, something she could get way too dependent upon. He helped her inside the car after the driver opened the door. She leaned back against the seat, rolling her head to stare at him.

"I'll call you later."

She blinked blindly at him, as if she couldn't focus. "I'll talk to you tomorrow. I'm going to take a shower and go to bed." She hesitated a moment. "Don't call Luc, either."

"Okay. If that's what you want."

It didn't matter what she wanted anymore. It just was what it was. She nodded, and he shut the door.

What she wanted was to escape from it all. Maybe she should pack up and move, not tell anyone where she was headed. Start a new life somewhere far away.

But she couldn't run from her problems. As much as she wanted to, she had to face the music.

However horrible the chorus.

Sixteen

A pregnant silence filled the church office. Sunlight trickled in through the windows. It was a dark morning, but Spencer couldn't breathe in the scenery. He glanced at the faces of the elders seated before his desk, his heartbeat thumping. What if they asked him to step down?

Your will, Father, not mine.

Mr. Paul Fontenot, the leader of the elders, adjusted his glasses and pinned Spencer to his chair with his stare. "I don't see how anything's changed, Pastor." He nodded to the five men sitting to his right. "We told you that we'd allow you to tell the congregation when you were ready."

Sweat glued the shirt to Spencer's back. "Sir, it's all starting to come out. The sheriff knows, his deputies, my operators . . . it's only a matter of time before the church members find out."

"And what do you intend to do about

that?" Mr. Fontenot quirked a bushy brow.

"I want to be the one to tell them."

"Then I'd suggest you plan to do so." Mr. Fontenot glanced at the calendar in front of him. "We have a guest pastor speaking this Sunday. How about next Sunday?"

"You realize you could have demands to replace me when I do."

Samuel Boudreaux snickered behind his mustache. "Wouldn't be the first time."

Oh, that was just what he wanted to hear. Mr. Fontenot cast a glare at his congregant before returning his focus to Spencer. "I think you'll be quite surprised at the reaction you'll receive." He held up his hand to ward off any comments. "But if it happens, we'll handle the situation as we feel is in the best interest of the church as a whole."

Which would mean the call for his resignation.

He refused to let disappointment curdle in his gut. It was all in God's hands, where it should've been all along.

Spencer swallowed and pushed to his feet. "Thank y'all for meeting with me this morning. Let me just say now that it's been a blessing to work with each of you."

"Sounds like you've already got it in your mind what the outcome will be."

Giving the lovable elder a smile, Spencer nodded.

Mr. Fontenot wagged a bony finger at him. "Don't second-guess God's will, boy."

"Yes, sir." He headed down the hall.

Spencer waved at the church secretary as he slipped into his private office. He'd prefer to be checking up on what Felicia was up to but he had a date he couldn't miss. Circled in red on his desk calendar read the words "wedding planning session — Luc & CoCo." No way would he push this appointment to the back burner.

Luc and CoCo had overcome so much adversity and problems. To see them now, happy and so in love, filled Spencer's heart with pure joy. Who knew, maybe if those two could make it despite the odds stacked against them, there might be hope for him and Felicia.

He cut off his thoughts and stared out the window. The sun had faded, and now dark clouds loomed heavy in the southern sky. The hint of rain whispered on the wind blustering over the bayou. A sign? Spencer shook off the ominous sensation settling over him.

Your will, Father God. I'd rather be asked to resign and be in Your will than to do what I love and be out of it. Forgive me for not trusting You.

Miller's had two fancy knife sets in butcher blocks. Felicia stared at them both, taking out a knife from each set and examining them. Too bad she didn't know what the knife found in Wes's car looked like. Still, either one of these sets was entirely too elaborate for a bachelor.

"Hey, Felicia. May I help you?"

Felicia glanced over her shoulder to find Anna Beth hovering. One of the drawbacks of living in such a small town — everybody knew everybody and their business. Made it a little difficult to do any sleuthing. Or, maybe not. She held up the knives. "Hi, Anna Beth. These are lovely. What can you tell me about them?"

"These are both nice sets." Anna Beth pulled one out from the butcher block. "This one in particular is a good seller. See the detail on the handle? Very nice touch."

"A good seller, huh?" Felicia sheathed the other knife with a scrape as it slipped into the wood. "But I don't want it to be so popular that everyone has this set, yes?"

"Oh, no. I don't think you have to worry about that. Most of these sets are ordered for special occasions, like weddings or anniversaries. Besides, we only started carrying them three months ago."

"Ordered?"

"My, we don't stock those expensive things. Both of those are special orders only. Were you looking for a wedding gift for your brother and CoCo?"

Well, she hadn't considered that, but maybe. . . . "Do they take a long time to come in?"

"Most times we get them within a week of ordering." Anna Beth replaced the knife into the block. "Would you like me to order you a set?"

"You just order it, and what, call me when it comes in?"

Anna Beth nodded. "Most times we have to fill out paperwork and have the customer pre-pay. So we don't get stuck with something we can't sell off the shelf, you understand. But I know you, so I can just order."

Paperwork! "You know what, Anna Beth? I think I will order a set. And it'd be so much easier on me to go ahead and do your paperwork and pay for it. Then I can just have someone come pick it up for me, yes?"

"Perfect. Do you know which set you prefer?"

Felicia tapped her chin. "Actually, is there any way you can check and see how many have been ordered in the past few months?

I'd want to order the one that's ordered the least. Wouldn't want CoCo to have a set that matches any of her friends."

Anna Beth nodded. "Good idea. Yes, we keep the record orders. *Allons* back to my desk, and we'll access the computer."

Missy popped her gum and stared as Felicia entered the station. "Need to see the sheriff?"

Felicia nodded. Better not to say anything. Everybody in Lagniappe knew the old saying — telephone, telegraph, tell Missy.

Sheriff Theriot arrived momentarily, his face scrunched into a disapproving stare. "What can I help you with, Felicia?"

"I need to talk to you." She tossed a nod toward Missy. "In your office, please."

He let out a sigh and opened the swinging door for her. "Come on back."

Once in his office, she dropped into a chair. "I'd like to talk to you about your arrest of Wes."

"As I've already explained, I'm not at liberty to discuss the case with you or anybody else."

"But about the knife."

He jerked his stare to hers. His held a sternness that darkened his eyes. "Let it go. We've done the investigating. The prosecutor's taking this to trial."

"Have you looked into the possibility that Wes may have been set up?"

The sheriff let out a groan. "C'mon, Felicia. You've watched too much television. Setups rarely occur. We have him on motive, means and opportunity. Don't forget we found the murder weapon in his car."

"His *unlocked* car. And where'd he get that knife, huh? Why's a bachelor have such an expensive knife? He didn't have the rest of the set when you searched his house, did he?"

"Probably got rid of them."

Felicia snorted. "But he kept the one with blood under the seat of his car? Please. And those things are pricey. I just ordered one for Luc and CoCo. Those sets are more than a hundred dollars."

"The Ellenders aren't exactly hurting for money."

"And, only Miller's carries them, and they have to be special-ordered and they only started carrying them three months ago. Anna Beth over there told me none of the Ellenders have bought a set."

The sheriff shook his head and scowled. "Didn't I warn you not to interfere in this investigation?"

"Interfere?" Felicia let out a half groan,

half snort. "If you were doing your job, I wouldn't have to."

Sheriff Theriot tossed his glasses onto the desk. "Listen to me, Felicia Trahan. I'm doing my job, and you're interfering." He shoved to his feet. "This is it. No more. If you do so much as make a phone call about this case, I'll arrest you quicker than a frog snaps a fly off a lily pad." He fisted his hands against the desk and leaned over, daunting and domineering. "Do I make myself clear?"

"I just can't stand that you have the wrong man behind bars."

He pointed a finger in her face. "That's not for you to decide. I'm telling you a final time, back off. We've got it handled."

She clenched her jaw, grinding her teeth. "Fine." She stood. "Just know you have the wrong man. The real killer's still out there. Live with that."

Felicia didn't even look at Missy as she left the station and slipped into the back seat of her car. Her driver remained silent as well. Probably texting and reporting her visit to Luc. She didn't care anymore. Right was right.

She didn't bother to say anything to the driver as she made her way into the physical therapy clinic. Today was a good day to work out. She needed to release some of her frustrations. Moving to the stationary bike, Felicia dumped her cane and went straight to warming up, not even waiting on Mark.

How dare the sheriff threaten her? She'd offered up good, sound investigative work. The *cooyon!* Maybe he was upset because she was doing his job for him? And better.

"Slow down and take it easy," Mark chided as he approached her.

Felicia wiped the sweat from her brow on her shirtsleeve. "Can't. Luc's wedding is coming up, and I'm determined to walk without that stupid cane." At least she had their wedding present taken care of. She shifted to the leg-press machine.

"You've skipped a couple of days, girl. You keep this pace up and you'll rip something."

He'd no sooner got the words out than a pop sounded in Felicia's left calf, followed by a sharp, searing pain. Dots of color danced before her eyes. She cried out and let the leg-press weight clank back to the base. Her eyes crossed as hot stabs spread throughout her lower leg.

Mark knelt at her feet and took her leg in his hands.

Even his gentle touch brought agony. The

211

gasp/groan escaped from her lips.

He ran his hands over her skin, his fingers probing the muscles.

Felicia laid back against the bench, crying as the pain threatened to make her pass out. Even the recovery after surgery hadn't hurt this badly.

He frowned. "I think you snapped a tendon."

She shoved to sitting. "One of the ones they operated on?" Please, not that. They'd have to go back in and reconnect it to the muscle if she had.

"I honestly don't know. We need to get you to the doctor."

The flatness of his voice scared her. All the warnings her physician had preached rang in her ears — *slow and steady, Felicia, and you'll have a complete recovery.* Now look what she'd gone and done.

"Can you stand?"

Mark helped her into a standing position. She kept all her weight on her right leg. "Try putting some pressure on the left leg."

As soon as just the tip of her toes made contact with the floor, throbbing pain shot around her calf, twice as intense as before. She cried and clung to Mark, who supported her entire weight as he led her to his car.

He sped toward the hospital, frequently glancing in his rearview mirror to meet Felicia's tear-filled stare. She clenched her jaw. The pain didn't subside. She inhaled deeply through her nose and exhaled slowly through her mouth. The sting just increased. She let out a whimper.

"Just try to keep it still. Your doctor said he'd meet you at the emergency room."

"Thanks." Through gritted teeth, Felicia tried to be strong, but the ache weakened her. The dancing spots returned. Beads of sweat popped up on her upper lip, feeling as if they weighed as much as a twelve-foot gator. Nausea stirred in her stomach. Numbing tingles spread across her chest. Darkness engulfed her.

Stabbing pain brought her upright.

Bright lights nearly blinded her as she blinked into awareness. Clattering and clanking echoed. She tried to move, but warm, gentle hands gripped her shoulders. "It's okay, Felicia."

Spence? How . . . what? She blinked faster, fighting for orientation.

"Shh. Relax. The doctor's looking at your X ray. You're supposed to keep still." His voice was as smooth as molasses syrup.

It all came back to her — overdoing it,

the popping, the pain, Mark driving her here.

She blinked a final time, and Spence finally came into focus. "Wh-what are you doing here? Where's Mark?" Her mouth felt as if cotton had been jammed down her throat.

"He had to get back to work. He called me. You passed out on the drive." Spence smoothed her hair from her face. "Gave him quite a scare, too."

"He called you?" Her brain still had cobwebs filling the blank spaces.

"Well, he tried Luc first, but got his voice mail. So, he got me at the center."

"Why?"

"I don't know. But I was only too glad to come."

The door swished open and Dr. Guard breezed in. "My, you were really trying to hurt yourself, weren't you, missy?"

Heat fanned her face. "How much damage?"

Dr. Guard raked his gaze over her. "You were lucky. Just a minor muscle torn."

"It doesn't hurt nearly as badly as before."

"Of course it doesn't. We've given you an injection of painkillers. You'll be dopey for the better part of this afternoon."

She licked her lips. "Will I need another

surgery?"

"At this point, we don't think so."

Relief flooded her and she smiled.

"However, young lady, I'm ordering you on complete bed rest for the next week. After that, we'll run some more tests and I'll see."

"Yes, sir."

Dr. Guard glared. "I mean it, Felicia. You so much as put your body weight on that leg and the tear can enlarge, which *will* mean another surgery. Or more."

She nodded.

"I want your promise. I don't like having you mess up my beautiful work." The doctor kept staring sternly, but his aging eyes twinkled.

"I promise."

He stared at her for a long moment, then nodded. "Good." He handed her a small vial with the logo of the hospital pharmacy. "These are your painkillers. Take one every six to eight hours. Call me if you have any problems, and I'll see you in my office next Friday at nine." With a final wave in her direction, the good doctor swept from the room.

"Whew. What a relief." Felicia scooted to the end of the examining table.

"Whoa, there. Let me help you." Spence

grabbed hold of her arm.

"Just hand me my cane. I know how to walk with it and not put any weight on my leg."

Spence glanced around the room. "Uh, I don't think Mark brought it."

"Lovely." No cane, no driver. She was batting a thousand. At least the painkiller seemed to work. Her leg still throbbed, but the pain had dulled.

"I'll swing by Mark's office and grab it for you."

"I don't want you to g—"

A nurse shoved open the door and pushed a wheelchair inside. Felicia became increasingly aware how small the room seemed with the added contraption. Or maybe it was the close proximity to Spence that made her feel almost claustrophobic.

No, it was the wheelchair. She'd lived in one all her life, save the past year. She'd worked hard, endured pain and agony to get out of the contraption, and now, here she faced being in one again.

Helpless. Crippled.

"Here we go. Let's get you into the chair. Your husband can bring around the car." The nurse locked the brakes on the wheelchair and moved to help Felicia.

"H-h-he's not my husband." Heat

scorched her cheeks.

The nurse placed her hands on her ample hips. "Well, I don't know why not, honey. He's a dream. And so concerned about you, too." She smiled at Spence.

He turned a delightful shade of red, lowered his head and mumbled that he'd bring the car around.

Felicia giggled, then clamped a hand over her mouth. What was wrong with her? Must be the medication.

The nurse found it amusing, as well, and Felicia was pretty certain she hadn't taken any painkillers. She helped Felicia into the wheelchair. "Didn't mean to embarrass your young man, but he is a looker, honey." She set Felicia's feet on the pads and unlocked the brakes. "Better hook that one before someone else does."

As the nurse rolled her down the hallway of the hospital toward the front exit, Felicia considered the woman's words. She'd found Spence attractive ever since she'd met him almost a year ago but had ignored the feelings as she'd been in raw mourning over Frank's death. Little by little, she and Spence had formed a friendship of mutual affection and respect. But over the past few weeks . . . well, she'd awakened to just how deeply her feelings for him truly ran.

She ignored the nurse's ramblings, trying to concentrate on the conflicting arguments going on inside her head. What about his past — the time he'd spent in prison for trying to kill a man?

He could've killed him, but he didn't.

He tried. Admitted he wanted to kill that man.

That man had raped and murdered his little sister. What would Luc have done?

He had kept it secret. Hadn't trusted anyone, not even her.

For fear of being judged. Hadn't he been right on that count?

He had lied.

Had he?

The automatic doors opened with a whoosh. Wind scattered dried leaves across the ramp.

"Gonna have some rain by nightfall," the nurse said.

As if on cue, thunder rumbled in the dark clouds.

Spence pulled his truck curbside, shot out of the driver's seat and opened the passenger door.

"Such a gentleman," the nurse clucked.

Yes, that he was.

Felicia let out a little groan as they moved her from the chair to the truck. The nurse

218

patted her good leg. "You remember what I told you, honey. Better get him off the market as quick as you can," she whispered before shutting the door.

Spence slipped back behind the wheel and glanced at her. "You okay?"

No words came. Mutely, she nodded.

"Want to run by and get your cane, or would you rather go home and lie down?"

Her heart wrenched. Such care and concern lined his face. His very handsome face. His gentle eyes. His strong jaw.

"You know what, you look wiped out. I'll take you home, get you settled, then go get your cane. How's that?"

As if she could answer? She nodded again.

He put the truck in gear, and they were off. Felicia laid her head on the headrest and closed her eyes, soaking in being with Spence.

Oh, merciful days, she loved him.

Her heart tripped. What was she supposed to do about that?

SEVENTEEN

Would she never stop needing someone to wait on her? Allowing Spence to carry her into her apartment served a large dose of humility to her fledgling pride.

"Want to lie on the couch or in your bedroom?" He wasn't even winded from carrying her.

Her face flamed. What was it with her embarrassment factor today? Something about the image of Spence tucking her into bed felt entirely too intimate. "On the couch, please."

He lowered her to the cushions — thank heavens CoCo had delivered them early this morning — and eased a pillow behind her back. "Let me get you a blanket or something."

"Hall closet."

The man's attentiveness did nothing to detract from the fact that she loved him. Now she needed to do some soul-searching and have a long talk with God to see what to do about it. "Spence, would you grab my Bible from the bedside table?" Luckily, it'd been in her purse when her place had been trashed.

He returned with her Bible and the double-wedding-ring quilt her grandmother had made before she passed.

Was God trying to tell her something?

After tucking the blanket around her legs, Spence handed her a yellow sweater. "This was in the closet. Thought you could use it."

She took the soft knit and drew it close to her chest. The sweater Jolie had asked to borrow the night she was killed. She slipped her arms into the sleeves and wove it tightly around her.

"Let me get you something to drink so you'll have it close."

"There's some bottled water in the icebox."

He disappeared and returned in a flash, toting two bottles of water. He set them on the coffee table and pulled it closer to the couch. In a flurry of activity, he grabbed the cordless phone and handed it to her, retrieved the extra throw pillow from the chair and slipped it behind her back, then brought her a package of crackers.

"I'll be fine." Felicia laughed, feeling the full effect now of the injection the doctor had given her.

"It shouldn't take me long to get your cane. Can I get you anything else while I'm out?"

"A new leg?" She let loose with a fit of laughter.

Spence stared at her as if she'd sprouted lichen. "Pain must not be too bad."

"Nah. This medicine seems to be working well enough."

"Better than that, I'd say." He smoothed down her hair, his fingers lingering as they brushed against her face.

She leaned into his touch. It felt so nice. So warm. She was so sleepy.

He jerked his hand away and coughed. "I'll leave the door unlocked so I can get back in. Is there anything else you need before I leave?"

Even her toes were warm and cozy. "How about a kiss goodbye?"

He froze, his body going rigid. If he hadn't looked so shocked and scared, Felicia would've laughed. "Never mind. Didn't mean to traumatize you." Her body felt as if it were humming. She closed her eyes.

Then blinked suddenly as his lips grazed against hers for only a heartbeat. He kissed her temples, the tip of her nose, and both her eyes.

Blood raced through her veins. Now her body not only hummed, it practically sang opera.

"I'll be back soon," he whispered.

She really wanted to read some Scripture while he was gone, but her eyes were too heavy. She set the Bible on the table and snuggled under the edge of the quilt. She had a final thought before sleep overtook her, which made her smile.

What would it be like to have Spence tuck her in like that every night for the rest of her life?

Br-rring! Br-rring!

Felicia jerked her head forward. Then immediately regretted it as the beginning pulsations of a headache ravaged her temples. She rubbed the aching area.

The phone rang again. She thought she'd been dreaming before. She snatched the cordless. "Hello."

"I just talked to Spence. Are you okay?" Luc's voice held a load of concern.

"I think so. Yeah."

"You don't sound so good. Why don't CoCo and I come over and bring you some supper?"

"No. I'm just groggy from the pain medicine. I was asleep when you called."

"I'm sorry for waking you."

"I'm okay. Really. I'll sleep off this pain-killer hangover."

"Bubba called me today as well. Heard you went and visited Wesley Ellender in jail on Sunday afternoon. Care to explain why?"

"Not particularly." Wow, Percocet — backbone in a bottle.

"*Boo,* I don't have to tell you that wasn't a smart move. Bubba's royally teed off. Said he has half a mind to charge you with interfering in a police investigation." Static sounded over the connection as thunder rumbled enough to rattle the living room windows.

"That'd be a neat trick. He's already arrested someone. As far as I can tell, he isn't investigating anymore, and that's a shame, because Wesley Ellender isn't guilty."

Luc let out a loud sigh. "They found the murder weapon in his truck."

"Which they were led to by an anonymous tip. *Allons,* you know it screams of a setup." Her head felt all cottony. "I'd think you'd be more understanding, considering Uncle Justin almost did the same thing to you."

"Aren't you being snappish?"

She closed her eyes. "I'm sorry, Luc. I'm tired, the painkillers are making everything

224

fuzzy and I just want to go to sleep."

"Bubba said you'd been digging into the origin of the knife."

She sighed deeply. "Somebody has to."

"He's following up on your lead, *Boo*. He's doing the best he can."

"While Wes sits in jail." She yawned, long and loud.

"I don't like you being there by yourself."

"Spence will be back in a few minutes. He went to get my cane." She squinted toward the clock on the wall, but couldn't make out the time. Looking to the window, she couldn't determine an idea of the time as rain battered against the panes. Had she slept through a storm?

"I know. Remember, I talked to him?"

"Yeah. Look, I'm gonna go back to sleep now. I'm really tired and my head hurts. I'll talk to you later, yes?"

"Okay. But if you need anything, you call me."

"Will do. Love you." She didn't wait for a reply but turned the phone off and let it slide to the coffee table.

Oh, her head hurt bad.

A loud clap of thunder rattled the mirror over the buffet in the foyer. Lightning stretched across the darkened sky. A chill settled over her. She inched down further under the quilt.

What time was it, anyway? How long had Spence been gone? She glanced at the coffee table. Where was the television remote? Oh, on the chair's side table. Not close enough. Probably just as well. Spence had probably only been gone a few minutes. Just long enough for him to get to his truck and call Luc. She smiled to herself. Two men cared about her.

Lightning slashed . . . an electric pole sparked . . . a loud crack drowned out the thunder rumbling. Spencer planted his foot on the brake. As if in slow motion, the pole broke and fell across the road, missing Spencer's truck by a couple of feet. The transformer sent sparks off like fireworks as flames shot up.

He slammed the gear into Reverse and punched the gas, getting his truck away from the fire that danced in the barrage of rain. Dialing 911 on his cell, he told Missy about the fire and its location. There was nothing more he could do but try to keep others from getting too close.

Staring into his side mirror to detect any cars topping the hill behind him, he pressed on his hazard lights and let out a slow breath. That'd been a close call, and the adrenaline continued to speed through his veins. The full-flavored aroma of homemade chicken and dumplings filled the truck's cabin. He glanced at the brown paper sack on the passenger's seat. Moisture rings crept up the side. Great. He'd spilled it when he'd slammed on his brakes.

He straightened the bag and groped for napkins in the console. Probably not a good idea to stop and get takeout, but he was sure Felicia would be hungry later. She definitely needed something in her stomach to absorb the pain medication. It'd made her downright loopy.

She'd asked him for a kiss.

Had to be the drug talking, not her.

He hadn't been able to turn down her request. Planting feathery kisses over her face had squelched any doubts he'd had that he was in love with her. Totally and completely. And he'd made up his mind — he would tell her. Whether she'd give him the boot or agree to date him, he didn't know.

But he'd find out.

After the painkiller wore off.

The sky behind him flashed red and white. He twisted in his seat to see the fire truck pull up parallel to his truck, splashing water from the road over his windshield. He stepped into the driving rain.

"What happened?" the tall fireman asked.

"Lightning hit it, I think."

The fireman nodded, his hat bobbing in the rain. "Happens a lot in these kinds of storms." He glanced at the smoldering transformer, then at Spencer's truck. "We'll take care of it from here. You can head on back."

Spencer shook his head. "I need to get down this road."

"Well, it'll take us some time to make sure the wires are dead. Then we'll have to cut the pole to get the road cleared. We don't have a saw on this rig, but we'll radio for one to be brought out."

"About how long?"

"Thirty minutes or so, after we get the saw."

Maybe he should backtrack. But no, going the long way around would take him about fifty minutes to get to Felicia's apartment. With the rain, who knew what other delays he'd encounter. "I'll wait."

The fireman nodded again. "Then back your truck up a couple hundred yards. We've already called the electric company to kill the feed here."

Spencer did as instructed, letting the heater stay on an extra minute or so after he moved the truck. The rain had soaked his clothes and the wind bit into him. Maybe he'd dry out a little before he got back to Felicia's. She'd probably get irked if he muddied up her floors.

He lifted his cell phone. Should he call Felicia and tell her he'd been delayed? He recalled her dazed expression. No, he wouldn't call. She probably crashed before he even got to the parking lot, and she needed her rest.

As the storm raged and the firemen worked, Spencer wondered how to broach the subject of his love to Felicia.

Bam! Bam! Bam!

Felicia shook herself awake and reached for the phone. If Luc was calling her back . . . She must've scooted the phone over the table because it lay just out of reach of her fingertips.

Bang! Bang!

Not the phone, the door. Didn't Spence remember he left it unlocked? She sat as upright as she could. Probably it was Luc and CoCo, despite her telling him she didn't want him to come over. She let out a groggy sigh. "It's open."

The door pushed open. Felicia opened her mouth to give Luc a good talking-to, only to let her jaw hang slack.

A young woman stood in the doorway. The one Felicia had talked to the other day by the Dumpster.

"May I help you?"

"I need to talk to you." The woman shut the door behind her and turned the dead bolt.

Why would the woman lock the door? Pinpricks of apprehension shot over Felicia. "Do I know you?" Her voice came out squeaky.

"Kinda." The woman moved across the room and plopped into the chair. The very wet woman in the new chair.

"I've seen you around here a few times. Do you live in the apartments?" Felicia felt like she was caught in some cross between a Stephen King movie and the *Twilight Zone.*

"Nope. Don't live here."

The pinpricks graduated to the size of lily pads. Felicia fought against the fuzziness of her mind. There was something she should remember about this woman. Something odd, different. But she couldn't remember; the medication dulled all her senses.

Finally like a rod being cast, Felicia remembered. The woman had mentioned Felicia's wheelchair when they spoke the other day.

No one in the complex knew she used to be wheelchair-bound!

Felicia's mouth felt as if she'd been eating sand. From the drug or fear, she didn't know. She leaned forward, throwing her full body weight toward the table and reaching for the phone. The edge of the table dug into her shoulder, mixing with the already-throbbing pain of her leg and head. The cordless skidded off the other side and landed on the floor with a loud thud.

Felicia shoved herself back to the couch, rubbing her shoulder.

The woman laughed. Callous cackling.

Felicia'd heard it before. Not when she talked to her before. Not here at the complex. Not at church. At work . . .

Winnie!

The last vestiges of confusion from the painkiller fled like a motorboat over water.

The woman laughed at Felicia as she lifted the phone and shoved it behind her on the chair. "I see you figured out who I am, princess."

Winnie shoved the coffee table away from the couch. Her eyes darkened and narrowed. "You and me, we need to talk."

EIGHTEEN

Those chicken and dumplings smelled mighty good right now. Wet and cold, Spencer knew a bowl would warm him right up. But he wanted to share supper with Felicia. He glanced at his watch. For forty-five minutes, the firemen had worked. They'd put out the embers and now waited on whoever was bringing the saw. The constant rain didn't seem to help matters.

He let out a long-suffering sigh. It probably would've been much faster if they'd allowed him to assist and just move the encumbrance into the ditch. No such luck when he'd made the suggestion. Policies and procedures. He gave a snort and stared at his cell phone.

What if Felicia had awoken and wondered where he was? Maybe he should call her and let her know he'd be on his way shortly. But what if she was still asleep? He didn't want to wake her.

What should I do, God?

He tapped his fingers against the steering wheel. What to do, what to do? He opened the phone and dialed Luc.

"Hello."

"Hey, it's Spence."

"You back at Felicia's?"

"Not yet. Lightning hit an electric pole and it went down over Highway 1. The firemen are clearing the road now."

"Anybody hurt?"

"Nope. I was the only one on the road."

"That's good."

"Has Felicia phoned you?"

"Nope. I called her after I talked to you. She sounded pretty out of it and said she was going back to sleep. Those painkillers must be knocking her for a loop."

How about a goodbye kiss?

Yeah, he'd say the medication wasn't allowing her to think clearly. "I was thinking maybe I should call and let her know I'm on my way."

"Any idea how much longer you'll be stuck there?"

"Probably another twenty minutes or so." If the other truck would ever show up with the saw.

"Then I wouldn't worry about it. She's probably still sleeping. She didn't even warm up to the suggestion of me and CoCo bringing her supper."

"Well . . ."

Luc laughed. "You got her something, didn't you?"

Spencer's face heated. "I thought chicken and dumplings might make her feel better."

Luc chuckled louder. "Man, you've got it bad."

"What?" Spencer white-knuckled the steering wheel.

"You're over the moon for her, aren't you?"

He worked his throat, trying to dislodge the lump sitting sideways. "Um, um . . ."

"Hey, man, been there, done that. I know how you feel."

"It's complicated."

Luc roared with laughter. "Pastor, when women are involved, it's always complicated." A rustling came over the line, followed immediately by an "ouch."

Spencer laughed himself. "CoCo nailed you?"

"Did she ever. Woman has a mean right jab. Tyson ain't got nothing on her." More rustling preceded another *ow!*

Spencer chuckled. "I'll let you go work that out." He struggled to see through the rain pelting the windshield. A second truck had appeared on the other side of the road, lights flashing. "I think they're about to be done here."

He closed his cell phone and blew into his cupped hands. Even talking to Luc didn't seem to alleviate the ominous feeling overcoming him.

Call her!

He snatched the phone and dialed her number. It rang four times, then went to her voice mail. Spencer left a brief message before closing the phone. Maybe she was just sleeping. But he'd given her the phone to keep with her. Why wasn't she answering?

His gut twisted. He didn't feel good about this. Not at all.

He stared at the firemen about to saw away at the pole.

Hurry!

Winnie held the now-silent phone in her hand, staring at the caller ID. "Bertrand, Spencer. That's the preacher man, right?"

Felicia nodded, the movement causing her head to pound in synch with her heart.

How'd Winnie find out where she lived, anyway?

"Well, we don't want to be interrupted, now do we?" Winnie slipped open the back cover of the phone and removed the battery. She tossed the battery onto the chair behind her and laid the phone on the table.

"Look, I don't kn—"

"Shh." Winnie smiled, revealing a row of perfectly straight and white teeth. She really was an attractive young girl. Except for her eyes. Dark rings of hatred surrounded her irises. "I don't want you to talk right now. You're gonna listen. That's what you do, right?"

Felicia bunched the edge of the quilt into a ball. *Lord, help me. This woman's crazy.* And with her bum leg, Felicia was helpless.

"You think you're so high and mighty, taking calls from people who have problems. You think you can solve everyone else's issues. Must be nice to be so perfect."

"I'm not perfect." Hardly. Especially now, when her body throbbed and fear seeped into every pore.

Winnie pointed and inched to the edge of the chair, leaning toward Felicia. "Uh-uh-uh . . . I told you not to talk. You're supposed to listen."

Anger mixed with the fear strangling her throat. Felicia snapped her lips together tightly. Where was Spencer? He should be back by now.

"What gives you the right to tell people

what to do? You just stick your nose in places it doesn't belong."

As if she'd answer when Winnie'd told her twice to keep silent. Felicia stared at the young woman unraveling before her eyes.

"You aren't any smarter than the rest of us, except you have a big mansion, have a limo, and you think that makes you better than me? Smarter?"

Felicia licked her lips. Dare she try to explain? By the look in Winnie's eyes, she'd do better to remain quiet. Why had she told Luc not to come over?

"Well, I'm smarter than all of you. All the stupid people here in Lagniappe and that idiotic *Christian* call center."

Biting the inside of her cheek, Felicia let her gaze leave Winnie while stiffening her back. She'd fought too hard to gain her independence. No knight in shining armor would be arriving to rescue her, so she'd better find something she could use to defend herself.

"What is it with y'all and God? He's a crutch. Something stupid people cling to instead of working out their problems."

Felicia refrained from reminding Winnie that she'd called a Christian crisis hotline for help.

The pillar candle? Would that work? Nah,

it'd probably just break.

"I've got news for you, sistah, God isn't real. He's a figment of the imagination."

"No, He isn't." The words escaped before Felicia could stop them.

Winnie narrowed her eyes. "I thought I told you to shut up. You don't pay attention very well, do you?"

Winnie shot out of the chair, towering over Felicia as she slapped her across the face.

Felicia laid a hand against her stinging cheek. Her skin was hot to the touch. Indignant tears burned her eyes.

Lord, please help me.

"Oh, you're gonna cry now?" Winnie laughed. "How priceless."

Blinking back the tears, Felicia refused to play into the woman's plan. She jerked her hand down and slipped it under the quilt. She wouldn't give in now. No way, no how.

Winnie cackled more. "Don't you get it, princess? You're at *my* mercy now."

Felicia wanted to ask how Winnie had ever been at her mercy, but with the heat still searing her cheek, she bit her lip. Her injured muscles tensed but she refused to flinch.

"That's right. You and me, we're gonna get some things straight. Like how you kept telling me I didn't want to really hurt anyone." Winnie snorted and stood. She paced, her words enunciating each step. "How do you know? Maybe I did want to hurt someone. Like my ex's new girlfriend. That hussy."

She turned and stared at Felicia, smiling like a gator about to snap a bird in its massive jaws. "She got what she deserved."

The sick feeling returned. Felicia had an idea it had nothing to do with the pain medicine, but more with the realization that she sat in a locked apartment with a deranged person.

Who seemed bent on making Felicia pay for whatever perceived wrong danced in Winnie's head.

Wrinkling her nose, Winnie continued pacing. "She came across as cute and bubbly. Sweet. Trying to be something she wasn't." Winnie grunted and rolled her eyes. "Yeah, right. Saccharine sweet, if you ask me."

Where was a good baseball bat when you needed it?

"And his dumb self fell for it — hook, line and sinker. Such a man. Waltz a short skirt in front of them with a little giggle, and they'll roll over for you."

Wasn't there an extra curtain rod under

the couch? Could Felicia grab it without Winnie noticing? Wait, it wasn't there anymore. They'd used it to replace the one broken in the last break-in.

"And, boy, did he roll over. Followed her as if he were some little schoolboy with a crush." She gave a humorless laugh. "Yeah, he's a rat, all right."

What about her cane? Felicia let her gaze fall to the areas beside the couch. Her cane was never out of arm's reach. Oh. Right. She was still a little fuzzy on details, but she remembered Spence had gone to get her cane from Mark's. Why wasn't he back yet? Surely enough time had passed.

"He just threw me away like a sucked-out crawfish head. After I'd already started filling my hope chest with linens and stuff for the day we'd be married." Pain edged into Winnie's words.

Maybe Felicia could use that pain. There sure wasn't anything she could use as a weapon of sorts. Except her intelligence. Hadn't she been able to talk Kipp down and get him away from her? She took a deep breath. "I know how you feel," she ventured.

Winnie jerked her stare from the window and glared. "What do you know about it?"

"I've lost a guy I dated before."

"He left you for someone else?"

Good, Winnie was talking. Now to just keep her communicating. Just like she had with Kipp.

"That wasn't the reason he gave, but he did eventually find someone else." Felicia backtracked through her memories to high school. "You see, I was in a wheelchair, and that was hard for most guys to deal with." It hadn't been for Frank.

Apparently not for Spence, either. He'd never treated her any differently before her surgeries.

"What happened?" Animosity momentarily forgotten, Winnie dropped to the chair. The way her mood seemed to flip back and forth so quickly . . . what was up with her?

"He stood me up for prom. I guess having a date who couldn't dance and was on wheels didn't sound appealing to him."

"How rude."

Felicia gave a slight smile. "I found out later his friends had dared him to ask me to prom. He'd never really wanted to go with me, anyway." All these years later, the truth still hurt.

"What'd you do?"

"Do? Nothing." Felicia gave a dry laugh. "You can't make someone like you if they don't." The rest of the memory filled her mind, and she laughed. "However, my big brother bloodied his nose."

Winnie laughed, too, then frowned. "At least you have someone to take up for you. I have to take up for myself."

"Actually, I was mad at my brother for doing that."

"Why? The dude deserved it."

Felicia shook her head. "I don't know why it happened, but I know it happened for a reason. Everything happens for a reason."

Winnie crossed her arms over her chest and smirked. "You're saying God had that guy stand you up and humiliate you as part of some big plan?"

Oh, Lord, give me the words.

"I believe so." Felicia tucked her hair behind her ear. "Maybe so I'd know what it felt like, to teach me compassion. Maybe so I'd recognize real love when I felt it." Like she had with Frank.

Like with Spence. Her heart twisted. Where was he? Had he been in an accident?

As if on cue, the phone in the bedroom rang. Winnie didn't seem to hear it. "Give me a break. That's all a load of baloney." Winnie popped back to her feet, looking angry again.

"It's true."

Winnie towered over Felicia, holding her

242

by the shoulders and shaking her until Felicia thought her teeth would rattle out of her head. "Shut up, shut up, shut up!"

It had to be a combination of an empty stomach, the pain medication and the jarring movement. Felicia leaned over and threw up.

All over Winnie's shoes.

NINETEEN

Still nothing but voice mail. Surely she couldn't be still asleep? Did the drugs knock her out completely? Spencer slammed the cell phone into the console and stared at it.

Ring. Call me back.

But it remained silent. He checked again to ensure the ringer was on and the volume set to high before tossing it back down.

Why wasn't she answering?

He glared at the firemen. How difficult could it be to saw a pole and chunk the bits into the ditch? Minutes felt like eons.

Time he didn't have.

His cell phone chirped. He jerked it up, not even bothering to check the caller ID. "Felicia?"

"Uh, no. It's Jon Garrison."

Spencer swallowed his groan. "What's up?"

"Called the center and Michael told me you'd taken the night off."

"Yeah." He wouldn't volunteer any additional information.

"Just reminding you we have an appointment tomorrow morning at nine."

As if he could forget. "I know."

"Okay. Don't be late."

"I won't."

"Who's Felicia?"

Should've known he wouldn't get off that easily. "One of the operators at the center."

"Mmm-hmm. Just an employee, huh?"

No more evasion. "She's a friend as well. She injured her leg post-surgery, and I'm just helping her out."

"Oh. Okay. Well, see you tomorrow."

Spencer snapped shut the phone. He could've gone into more detail with Garrison, but there wasn't any point. Not until he knew where he stood with Felicia.

He stared at the phone he still held.

C'mon, Felicia, call back.

Yet the phone remained stubbornly silent and still. Maybe he should call Luc and ask him to go check on her.

No, she'd been determined to not lean on her big brother anymore.

But what if something was wrong? What if she'd fallen and needed help?

He flipped open the phone.

Come on, Luc, pick up. But the phone

rang two more times, then directed the call to voice mail. What kind of message could he possibly leave that wouldn't panic her brother? None. He closed the phone, wondering who else he could call. No one.

He dropped the cell into the console as *tings* sounded on the truck roof. Staring out the windshield, he watched gumball-size hail pelt the firemen. The wind whirled, making a hissing sound. Another sign?

More of a delay. The firemen huddled closer to their truck. One lifted a radio to his mouth.

Spencer's insides felt as if someone grabbed them in a tight grip. He couldn't get hold of Luc to rush to her apartment, but he needed to check on Felicia. Now.

Decision made, Spencer turned over the engine, put the truck in Reverse and maneuvered in the limited space to turn around. It'd take him some time to backtrack, but at least he'd feel like he was making progress. Better than sitting and waiting.

If only he could shake the feeling that something was wrong.

Hail mixed with rain, making visibility close to zero. He crept along, the speedometer not reaching twenty miles per hour. He couldn't take a chance on slipping off the road or running into another delay. Cranking the defroster to high, Spencer arched over the steering wheel, his fingers digging into the worn cover.

"Stupid! Look what you've done." Winnie jumped back, nearly falling over the coffee table. She stared at her shoes as if a water moccasin had just writhed between her feet.

"I'm sorry. I'm not feeling well. It's the medicine." Felicia wiped her mouth with the back of her hand. The room continued to spin. Why'd she ever pick out such loud and vibrant pieces of art? They all melded together in a psychedelic blend — a spinning, nausea-inducing blend.

Winnie glared. "You threw up on me."

Why not state the obvious? "I didn't mean to." Her voice came out as weak as Felicia felt. And her stomach continued to roll like a wave over the bayou.

Winnie jerked Felicia's arm. "Get into the bathroom, idiot."

"I can't. My leg." Felicia refused to move. She kept her injured leg propped on the couch, even though Winnie almost held her in a levitating position. Her arm would be ripped from the socket at any moment.

"Don't lie to me." The old Winnie was back in control. The violent lunatic.

Felicia yanked her arm free, anger spurring on her words. "Do you think I'd have laid here and let you slap and shake me if I could get up?" She pressed a hand against her forehead. The pounding got louder. "I can't put any weight on my leg."

"Stop sniveling. Get up." Winnie grabbed hold of her arm again, jerking harder this time.

Snatching free, Felicia glared. "I'm not sniveling, and I can't get up. Don't you get it? Are you that stupid?"

Rage brightened Winnie's cheeks.

Uh-oh. Might not have been the smartest thing to do, insulting her. But Felicia couldn't help it. Her head hurt, her leg ached, the nausea wouldn't go away and she worried about Spence. He'd called a good fifteen minutes ago, at least, yet he hadn't shown up. Something was wrong. And she was beyond tired of this woman who'd barged in and bullied her.

"How dare you!"

Felicia glanced up in just enough time to dodge the fist Winnie threw. Missing her target only enraged her more. Grabbing Felicia's shoulder to keep her in place, Winnie reared back her arm, fist balled. Felicia grabbed the edge of the quilt and flung it over Winnie's head. The fist flung wildly, but missed her.

Shoving Winnie backward over the coffee table with a loud crash, Felicia almost lost her balance. She swayed, using the back of the chair for balance. Hobbling, she made her way around the end table, heading for the bedroom. The door had a lock — she could make a 911 call from the extension.

No such luck.

Winnie grabbed her bad ankle. Felicia screamed as pain tightened her muscles. She fell to the floor in a heap.

Pain knifing up her leg stole her breath.

Her head jerked backward so hard, white dots went in and out of focus in front of her eyes. Facing the floor, she reached behind her and tried to grab her hair away from Winnie, who only pulled harder. Chunks of hair had to come out with the last yank. Tears blocked Felicia's vision.

The agony. Every part of her body throbbed, each crying out for relief.

No! She wouldn't allow herself to be beaten. She'd keep fighting.

God, please help me. Give me strength.

Felicia ignored the pain in her head and struggled to flip to her back. Winnie leaned over her, hand still woven into Felicia's hair. Felicia kicked her in the stomach with her good foot. Winnie let out a hard *oomph* and let go.

Scooting on her backside, Felicia moved out of Winnie's reach. She scrambled to stand, hopping on her good foot, and headed for the hallway.

A fist connected to her side. Hard. She leaned against the wall and slid to the floor.

"Oh, no, you don't. I'm not done with you yet, princess." Winnie grabbed her upper arm and jerked her to a stand. "You've caused me enough trouble."

Felicia teetered, her center of balance totally off kilter. All energy spent, she leaned heavily against Winnie, who walked her back to the living room and shoved her onto the couch. Landing hard, Felicia clenched her jaw against the pain.

Winnie rubbed her hip and scowled at the coffee table. "You broke it. Don't try to blame it on me."

The woman had assaulted her, and she worried about being blamed for a broken table? She was certifiable.

"You attacked me." And she hadn't been able to stop the raving maniac. Once again, Felicia cursed her disease and helplessness.

Winnie turned her scowl to Felicia.

Uh-oh. Bad move again. When would she learn to just keep her big mouth shut? Stop infuriating the raving mad lunatic.

Lord, I pray You'll give me wisdom and

strength. I really need it right now.

Using conversation had worked, for a bit. Maybe it would again. Felicia sucked in a deep breath, situated herself more comfortably on the couch, and turned on her most sincere smile. "Look, I don't know how we got off track. Let's both calm down and talk about this. Whatever your beef is with me, let's work to resolve it, yes?"

Winnie hesitated a moment, then sat in the chair. While her stare was still hard, at least she wasn't coming out swinging.

Whispering a prayer of thanks, Felicia considered her options. She couldn't give in to panic or fear. She could either play nice and try to find out the root of Winnie's problem or she could take the defensive and see if she could get away from her.

Not much of a choice, really. Injured, she wasn't much of a match for Winnie. Escaping from Winnie would have to be moved to plan B. Only to be put into play if absolutely necessary.

Felicia prayed her words would find a welcoming spot in Winnie's heart. "Why don't you really tell me why you came to see me?"

Wow, when had her voice become so calm and steady?

It must have impressed Winnie as well,

because the woman lost her angry look. She let out a soft sigh. "You betrayed me."

Felicia's heart took another twist. Just what she'd told Spence, but he hadn't listened to her. Why hadn't she fought harder? These poor callers depend upon their identity and problems remaining anonymous. Felicia cleared her throat. "It wasn't my call to make. We have to look at the overall picture, and at the time, the police were looking into everything at the center."

Winnie's arched her brows. "Really? Why's that?"

Maybe if she shared the truth, Winnie would understand. "One of our operators was murdered. The police were looking into a possible connection between her and any of the calls she'd taken."

She had Winnie's complete attention now. "Does that happen a lot? People threatening y'all?"

"No. But when it does, we have to notify the police."

"Hmm." Winnie rested her elbows on her knees, studying Felicia. "And did they find anything?"

"No. The police arrested her boyfriend."

"That Wesley Ellender I saw on the news?"

Felicia swallowed hard. "Yes."

"And the police found the knife with him, right?"

"Yes."

While Winnie pondered that, something niggled against Felicia's mind. Something off. She shoved away the feeling, wanting to keep Winnie talking rationally. Anything to buy her more time. Time to come up with something to get her out of the apartment. Or at least away from Felicia.

"Wonder if he'll get the death penalty." Winnie spoke more to herself than Felicia.

"I don't know. So, you see, I didn't want to betray you. I didn't have a choice."

Winnie snapped back to the conversation and narrowed her eyes. "Whose decision was it?"

A choking sort of fear scooted down Felicia's spine. "Well, the sheriff asked for any and all call records from people who'd been showing signs of aggression."

"That pastor guy, he's the one who ratted me out, wasn't he?"

"No, the sheriff had a warrant."

Winnie gave a snort and bounced to her feet. "Whatever. I should have known not to trust a man."

This was going down the wrong path way too fast. She'd better do something or she'd be running for her life again. "It doesn't matter now, Winnie."

"You don't think?"

Felicia forced a smile on her face. "No. Now, why don't you tell me about your ex?"

Winnie flashed those pearly whites of hers. "Let's just say he's indisposed."

TWENTY

Hurricane season was still months away, but it seemed no one had filled the wind in on that fact. It whipped and cut through downtown Lagniappe like a current in the channel. Mardi Gras decorations marched across the roads and lawns. It was downright eerie to see comedy/tragedy masks cartwheeling from the storm.

Spencer wiped his watering eyes. Straining to focus had made them ache. If only he could drive a little faster. At this speed, the route would take another ten to fifteen minutes to reach Felicia's. He inched down on the accelerator.

Should he try calling again?

He reached for the phone. His truck hydroplaned and fishtailed, the hood heading for the ditch. Spencer jerked his hand back to the wheel and steadily brought the truck under control. Water splashed against the undercarriage. Tires sung against the drenched pavement.

Thank you, Lord.

The snail's pace antagonized him, but he couldn't risk picking up speed. He wouldn't be much help to Felicia if he got in an accident. Grinding his teeth, he drove as slow as a snake in winter.

His phone rang. He jerked it from the console, never taking his eyes from the road. "Hello?"

"Pastor? This is Sheriff Theriot."

"Yes?"

"I just wanted to let you know Felicia hit on something."

"What?"

"Those knives. They *are* rather expensive. Miller's has gotten us a list of all the orders of people who purchased them in the past three months."

"And?" Spencer didn't need to play guessing games while he drove.

"Felicia was right. None of the Ellenders have bought them."

"So, what are you telling me?"

"We're still talking to everyone on the list, checking and making sure they have the complete set of knives."

"But?"

"There's a chance she might be right. Wesley could be innocent."

"And if he is?"

"Then we go back to square one. That means there still might be a link between the murder and your center." The sheriff paused. "And that means he's still out there."

All the more reason to get to Felicia and check on her. The killer could still be on the loose.

Indisposed? Did that mean dead?

Felicia clutched her hands in front of her and watched Winnie silently pace. The silent part worried Felicia. As long as Winnie talked, there was a hope, no matter how small, that this situation could end calmly. Even if Winnie ranted and raved and acted like a lunatic, at least she was communicating. But now . . . silence hovered in the room like a peeping Tom.

Besides the worry, Felicia wanted answers. "How, exactly, is he indisposed?"

Winnie plunked onto the edge of the chair and grinned. A wicked expression, really. "He's just, uh, unavailable right now. Probably for a long time to come, too." She laughed that callous cackle of hers.

It unnerved Felicia. Something lingered just outside the fuzzy edges of Felicia's memory. Some detail Winnie had said that struck a chord. What? She'd already recalled Winnie had slipped up about the wheel-chair. No, that wasn't it. Some important point.

If only she could remember.

Another memory invaded her. Spence's goodbye kiss. Actually, kisses. All over her face. Her heart flipped as she recalled how deep her love for him ran when he'd kissed her.

"What're you smiling about?"

Felicia jerked her thoughts back into line. How could she have been daydreaming in such a situation? Must be the painkillers. She snapped her full attention to Winnie. "I'm not. I'm wondering why you're being so cagey, yes? Why don't you just spit out what you did to him?"

Winnie laughed again. "I don't think so. It goes much deeper than your approval, prin-cess."

What couldn't she remember? What had Winnie said . . . something she commented on?

"Deep enough that you could face legal actions if anyone found out? Is that really why you're mad? Because the center noti-fied the police about your plans for re-venge?"

Laughter fled from Winnie. "Like I'd tell

258

you if that were right?"

"I'd hope so. I mean, coming here, attacking me, holding me against my will . . . don't you think that's illegal?"

The darkness returned to Winnie's stare. "Good point, princess."

Great. She'd gone and done it again — let her mouth overload herself. She'd better think fast or she'd be up a swamp with no airboat.

"But, not if nobody ever knows."

Winnie crossed her arms over her chest. "Oh, and I'm supposed to believe you won't tell anyone?"

"If I give you my word I won't, then I won't."

"Like my calls to you at the center weren't supposed to be discussed with anyone else?"

Oops, Winnie had her there. What was it Luc always preached — the best defense is a strong offense?

"You were threatening bodily harm to someone. We had no choice. I've already explained the situation." As soon as she said the words, she realized how ridiculous that argument sounded. Winnie had already done more to her than merely threaten her with bodily harm. "That decision was out of my hands. This one isn't."

"Forgive me if I don't believe you." She

shook her head. "Past experience and all that, ya know?"

Distract her. That was Felicia's only chance.

"I'm really curious. How'd you get revenge?" She noted the scowl twisting on Winnie's forehead. "Oh, don't tell me about the ex if you don't want to. I'm wondering about his new girlfriend. The one who stole him from you." Felicia's words tumbled over themselves. "I know you said she left. How'd you manage that?"

"I'm very resourceful when I need to be."

"I'm sure you are. Still, the information might come in handy. Just in case a guy dumps me again." No way would Winnie buy such a load of lies. Better think fast, something else to keep her talking.

But Winnie surprised her by sitting back on the chair. "You'd never be able to take it to the extremes I did."

"Try me. I'm more determined than I look." Felicia jutted out her chin in the way Luc always claimed showed off her stubborn streak.

Winnie snorted and rolled her eyes. "Not hardly, princess. You work at a crisis center, for pity's sake."

Score two for Winnie. But Felicia was still in the game. Winnie hadn't gone berserk

260

again. The talking was working. She just had to keep at it.

Until what? Someone showed up to save her?

No, she couldn't depend on anyone. She'd made too much of a fuss for anyone to try to take care of her. Had she shot herself in the foot with her demands to be left alone?

And then the lights flickered in the apartment.

Lights down the street extinguished with a pop.

Great. On top of everything else, a blackout. Spencer slowed his truck to less than five miles per hour. His headlights pierced the darkness. No vehicles approached. No lights glimmered in his rearview. The sensation of being totally alone almost smothered him.

He pulled into the apartment's parking lot and let out a long sigh of relief. Muscles in his neck bunched and twisted. He secured the bag of food under his arm, slipped out of his truck and stepped into water that covered his feet. Ducking his head against the driving wind and rain, he ran toward the walkway.

His shin made contact with something hard and unyielding, leaving him sprawled across the concrete. The bag flew across the courtyard and landed with a splat.

Spencer rolled to his back, gripping his smarting shin. So dark out here . . . what had he run into? He pushed into a sitting position and groped about in the darkness. Sure didn't want to chance hitting the unrelenting object again.

His hand made contact with cold metal. He ran his hand along the metal, gauging it to be about two feet high and not even a foot in front of him. Using the object as support, he pushed to his feet. He steered clear of the offending thing, veering left on his way around the corner.

Gait slowed by the ache in his shin, Spencer felt along the walkway. He counted the doors to Felicia's.

One.

Wind pushed sheets of rain against him.

Two.

Sirens screamed off in the distance. Pressure brakes of large trucks hissed from the road.

Three. Only two more doors to go.

Hiss!

Something rubbed against his sore shin. He jumped back and slipped on the slick concrete. His feet flew out from under him. He landed on his rear with an agonizing thud while water splashed up in his face.

Meow.

Stupid cat. Jumping out at him like that.

"Here, kitty, kitty, kitty," an elderly woman called out over the wind.

Kitty? The thing was a nuisance. A threat to society, creeping up on unsuspecting citizens in the dark.

The cat gave a final hiss and brushed past him. Spencer dug his fingers into the brick wall and pulled himself to his feet. Now his tailbone joined his shin in vying for his attention. Pain was a great motivator.

In the pitch blackness, disorientation came easily. Had he already passed the third door when he fell? Or had it been the fourth?

Beams of light shot into the sky. Electric company workers searching for the source of the outage.

Now he remembered. He ran his hand along the wall again. Four.

An unusual smell ripped by on the wind. Like burning rope. Oh, no, he prayed the power outage wasn't due to fire. His determination to get to Felicia increased tenfold.

Five.

Spencer edged toward Felicia's door. He didn't want to alarm her, but if she wasn't answering the phone . . .

He'd left it unlocked.

With rain-slicked hands, he grabbed the knob and turned.

Twenty-One

The doorknob rattled.

Thunk!

Felicia groaned against the weight in her lap as Winnie climbed on top of her and wrapped an arm around Felicia's neck. "What're you up to?"

"It's a power outage. From the storm," Felicia croaked. Winnie's forearm dug into her throat, nearly cutting off Felicia's breath. Felicia tugged, using her nails.

Winnie released her and dropped her voice. "Stop clawing me. And be quiet."

"Get off of me." Felicia shoved Winnie as hard as she could. A bump sounded against the coffee table.

The door rattled again.

"What's that?" Winnie asked in a whisper.

"I don't know. Maybe the wind hitting the door? I have a candle on the end table and matches in the drawer."

"Don't you try anything funny."

Felicia let out a snort and shifted down to the end of the couch. She fumbled in the dark for the drawer handle, got a hard grip and yanked it open. The drawer crashed to the floor. Loose items rolled across the hardwood floor as the drawer's contents scattered.

"What're you doing?"

"I dropped the drawer." Felicia lowered herself to the floor, taking care not to hit her injured leg, and felt around.

Lipstick. No, Chapstick. She spread her hands to the right.

A pad of sticky notes. A pen. Breath mints?

Pounding against the door. A neighbor? Who would come out in this weather?

"Felicia. Are you okay? It's Spence."

Hope shot through her until a strong jerk of her hair snapped her head back. Felicia groaned.

"Don't move and don't you dare say a word. Let him think you aren't here," Winnie grated against Felicia's face.

"He knows I'm here. I've got a hurt leg, remember?"

"Then stay quiet and light the candle." Winnie's hand tangled in Felicia's tresses.

"I'm trying to find the matches."

Winnie dropped beside her, still keeping a tight hold of Felicia's hair but with less force. Items shifted on the floor. Winnie shoved something into Felicia's hand. "Here."

A lighter? How'd a lighter end up in her drawer? She didn't smoke.

"Felicia. Answer me." Spence's voice rose above the raging the storm.

"I'll let you go just long enough to light the candle. Try anything and I'll slice you worse than your curtains," Winnie hissed.

Felicia maneuvered back to the couch and groped for the pillar candle. She located the tall column of wax and reached to flick the lighter over the wick, then hesitated. Revelation dawned on her. Slicing — knife!

The police hadn't ever mentioned Jolie had been stabbed to death. That news hadn't been available to the media. But Winnie had said "knife" when they'd talked about Wes being arrested.

How did Winnie know? And how'd Winnie know Felicia's curtains had been sliced to shreds?

An anonymous female caller had phoned the center and told Jolie that Wes had been with Sadie. An anonymous tip to the police had told them about the knife hidden in Wes's car. Did Winnie know Wes?

More pounding on the door. "Felicia, I'm going to break down this door if you don't answer me right now."

Her mouth felt gummy. The only way Winnie could know those things was if she . . . she was the killer and the intruder! Felicia fisted her hand, the lighter digging into her palm.

Winnie murdered Jolie!

No, it couldn't be. Winnie didn't know Jolie. But how else . . . ?

"What's taking so long?" Winnie's hand gripped Felicia's leg. Her sore leg.

She cried out and jerked her leg from Winnie's grasp.

"Felicia! I'm coming in." Panic laced Spence's words.

Winnie grabbed Felicia by the arms and dragged her down the hall, bumping into furniture and walls along the way.

"Spence, help!"

Winnie released her long enough to smack her upside the head. Felicia let out a scream and clawed at Winnie's face. Winnie slapped away her hand and continued down the hall.

A loud thump rammed against the door, followed by a grunt.

"The dead bolt's locked. Call the police," Felicia shouted.

Winnie rewarded her with a fist to the jaw.

Felicia's head whipped to the side. Stinging crept from her jawbone up her check and down her neck. The tangy taste of copper filled her mouth. She pressed a hand to her mouth. When she pulled it away, sticky moisture coated her hand.

Winnie flung them into the bedroom and slammed the door shut. In the dark, she fiddled with the knob. The lock turned with a resounding click. Seconds later, hot breath blasted against Felicia's face. "Now we won't be bothered."

Fear didn't seep into her bloodstream like Felicia expected. Instead, hope sprung forth. Spence would call the police, and in a matter of minutes, they'd be knocking down her door. She just had to distract Winnie long enough. And she had a distinct advantage — she knew the layout of her bedroom. In the dark, Winnie wouldn't see the nooks and crannies.

She tried to scoot to the bed, but Winnie grabbed her. "Where do you think you're going, princess?"

Tendrils of wind thrashed outside the window, making a hissing sound. The thick smell of rain hung over the air, even inside the apartment. Felicia inhaled deeply, drawing in strength.

"I'm trying to get my leg out of its awkward position. You dragged me, yes?"

Winnie loosened her hold. "Do you have

a flashlight or candle in here?"

"No. When you trashed my place, you broke them all."

"Oh." Then the air whooshed from Winnie. "Figured it out, did ya, princess?"

"That you broke into my place and ripped it to shreds? Oh, yeah, I got that." *Figured out that you killed Jolie, too.* But she wouldn't share that bit of information just yet. "I just don't understand why."

The bed ruffle rustled as Winnie moved. Felicia tested the area toward the bathroom with her other hand. No contact. So, Winnie'd shifted toward the window. Felicia held her breath and scooted about two feet toward the bathroom.

It, too, had a lock.

"What's that pastor doing out there?"

"Calling the police, I'm sure," Felicia said loudly. Maybe Winnie wouldn't notice Felicia had moved farther away. "What're you going to do?"

"I'm thinking," Winnie snapped. Her voice sounded as if she stood by the window, a good distance from the bathroom door.

Felicia chanced another scoot. Two more feet.

"You're so much more trouble than you're worth. Always stirring up more problems for me. It's always something. Even my so-called friend called the center to warn that hussy, but it was already too late."

The cry of sirens shouted into the dark night.

"The game's up, Winnie. You'd better concentrate on escaping." Another foot to the bathroom without detection.

"Shut up." Fabric swished. "Does this window go up all the way?"

Felicia hesitated. She wanted to get away from Winnie, but she also wanted the police to catch her. Besides, she was almost in the bathroom. Her hand pressed against the cold ceramic tiles. "Sometimes it catches."

"Let me see if it's locked." More fabric moving.

Bam! Bam!

Winnie gasped. The mattress squeaked as weight landed on it.

Sucking in air as well, Felicia scooted herself into the bathroom. She leaned to close the door, but it stuck against the rug.

"Felicia! Can you hear me?" Spence shouted from the window. "Can you hear the police? They're coming. Hold on."

Sure enough, the sirens were louder.

"I need to get rid of him. He's a nuisance," Winnie mumbled more to herself than Felicia. The mattress creaked.

271

Would Winnie find something to hurt Spence? Felicia's heart twisted. Forget locking herself in the bathroom until the police got here — she had to do something to protect Spence. She couldn't just hide anymore. "Like you did Jolie?"

"What?" Footfalls on the rug. A jarring of the dresser. Clanks and bumps as Winnie groped about. Looking for a weapon?

"Felicia. Where are you? I'm going to break the window."

"You mean, get rid of him like you did Jolie?" What could she use to protect Spence? She couldn't reach the medical scissors in the medicine cabinet.

"She took my man. My Wesley."

Felicia felt sick. No, she had to concentrate. Had to find a weapon of sorts.

"So, you put the knife in his car and called the police, all to get revenge on him for dumping you?"

"I'm about to throw a rock in. Move out of the way," Spence yelled.

Rustling, scraping and *oomphing* drowned out Spence's voice. Winnie must've lodged something against the window.

Sirens blared close. No more than a block away.

Think. Think. Think.

"I tried to warn him she was bad news.

But, nooo. He had to fall in love with her."
Winnie's voice drew closer. "She had to pay.
And when he wouldn't give me the time of
day after she'd died, well, I had no other
choice but to set him up. He'll spend the
rest of his miserable life in jail."

The shattering of glass echoed in the
storm, but Felicia didn't hear the sound of
a single shard falling to the floor of her
room.

"I had no intention of hurting you. I even
made that hussy take off that sweater you're
wearing before I killed her. See, I didn't
want to hurt you. I brought the sweater back
when you were moving and snuck inside
your old apartment and hung it up in the
closet. Worried you might not find it, but
you did. I know it's expensive. She had no
business wearing your stuff. Trying to make
herself look like something she wasn't.
Always using your expensive stuff to lure
Wesley. And then you go and thank me like
you did. . . ."

Footfalls off the rug, to the floor and onto
the carpet. Heading toward the bathroom.

Felicia tightened her fist. Something lay
inside. The lighter! She'd forgotten she'd
held it.

"You had to go looking into those knives.
Anna Beth mentioned the sheriff had come

by and pulled her list. He's been questioning people who ordered them. Wanting to
see their sets to make sure one isn't missing. I couldn't have that, now could I?"

Barely able to reach the edge of the
counter with her fingertips, Felicia grabbed
the aerosol can of hairspray.

The footsteps came closer. Almost to the
bathroom.

Felicia fumbled to find the hole on the
nozzle with her fingernail. She pointed it at
the doorway, the lighter in position in her
other hand.

Soles hitting the tiles with a squeak.

"I'm not in the mood for hide and seek,
princess."

Felicia flicked the lighter and pressed the
nozzle.

From his position outside the window,
Spencer watched as orange illumination lit
up Felicia's bedroom like a fireworks show.

A woman shrieked in pain.

Worrisome chills raced down his spine.
Spencer hammered harder with the rock,
freeing the glass from the window. A piece
of wood was wedged against the inside of
the frame. He stood on tiptoe and shoved.
Hard.

The orange light disappeared.

Sirens screamed close. The splashing of tires against water rang out, followed by the slamming of car doors.

The woman hollered again. Louder. Then the cry trailed off and silence prevailed. Not even a whimper.

Spencer knocked the wood from the window. "Felicia!"

"I'm okay." Her voice sounded weak.

"Sheriff. Open up!" They could hear Sheriff Theriot's voice at the front door.

"Spence, I'm okay, but I can't make it to the front door."

"I can climb in through the window. Hang on."

He gripped the sill, ignored the glass cutting into his palms, and pulled his weight up and over the ledge. He crashed to the bed, rolling as he landed. The stench of burnt hair and something else vile filled the room.

The lights shot on with a hum. Illumination chased the corners of the apartment. Windows in neighboring apartments glowed.

Bolting to the floor, he spied Felicia crumpled against the bathroom wall.

A woman, he couldn't guess her age, lay on her back on the threshold. She writhed and moaned, her hands to her head.

Her eyebrows were gone, her flesh bore scorch marks.

TWENTY-TWO

Spencer's mouth gaped. His eyes widened to the size of silver dollars. He stood rooted to the spot.

Felicia dropped the lighter and can of hairspray. "Spence."

No response. He didn't even look at her.

Felicia pulled to standing using the bathroom door. "Spencer!" She slapped her palm against the wood.

He gave a shake and met her stare.

"I'm okay. Go let the sheriff in the front door before he busts it down. Tell him to call for an ambulance."

He nodded but didn't move.

"Go!"

Her yell broke him from his trance, and he ran toward the living room. Felicia knelt beside Winnie. She grabbed the woman's hands, not letting her touch her burnt face again. "Shh. An ambulance will be here in a minute. Just be still."

Winnie moaned and cried. "You did this."

"I had no choice." Regret nearly choked Felicia. She'd never harmed another human being in her life. Tears welled in her eyes. "I'm so sorry."

The sheriff and Deputy Anderson stormed into the room, guns drawn. They took in the sight before them and holstered their weapons. The deputy took hold of Winnie's hands.

Spence returned to Felicia's side, pulling her into a hug. "I was so scared for you."

"I'm okay. It's Winnie I'm worried about."

"Winnie?" He cast his gaze to the woman lying on the floor, still writhing and bucking against the pain.

Felicia smoothed the singed hair from the woman's face. "Yes. This is Winnie."

Sheriff Theriot, with his notebook in hand, squatted beside them. His movements were slow. "Want to tell me what's going on here?"

"She needs an ambulance. Did you call for one?" Felicia asked.

He nodded. "They'll be here in less than three minutes, now that the roads are cleared." He touched Winnie's shoulder. "Ma'am, try to be still. Paramedics are on their way."

Winnie rolled and curled into the fetal

position. She struggled against the deputy's hold on her wrists.

The sheriff stood, nodding at Spence and Felicia to stand as well. Spence lifted Felicia easily with his arm around her waist.

"I need some answers here, Felicia." The sheriff waited.

Felicia licked her lips. They felt cracked and chapped. "This is Winnie, the woman who's been calling me at the center. The one we told you about."

"Go on," he instructed.

Spence tightened his hold around Felicia. She leaned against his muscular body, drawing strength. "She's also the woman who killed Jolie and broke into my house."

A siren's shriek drowned out the sheriff's and Spence's combined gasp.

Once the paramedics had taken Winnie into the ambulance, the sheriff led Felicia and Spence into the living room. He prompted Felicia to give an action-by-action replay of the night's events. Then he asked more questions. "Who, exactly, is this woman?"

"Winnie. She's Wes's ex-girlfriend. The one he broke up with before he began dating Jolie."

Spence laced his fingers with hers and squeezed. "Now it makes sense."

"So, you're telling me that young woman killed Jolie because of a man?" The sheriff wore a skeptical scowl.

"Felicia?"

"Yes. She was jealous of Jolie because Wes had become serious with her. Winnie couldn't take it."

He grunted and made notes in his little book. "And she just told you this? Confessed to everything, just like that?"

"Not exactly. I figured it out because she knew the murder weapon was a knife, and no one knew that."

Spence scooted closer to her on the couch until his outer thigh pressed against hers. She squeezed his hand. "I called her on it, and she admitted the truth. Then she told me I'd made more problems for her by telling you about the knife sets at Miller's. Anna Beth told her you'd pulled the order list for the past six months and were questioning everyone who bought one."

The sheriff's cheeks flamed. "You made a good argument."

Despite the heaviness of her heart, Felicia smiled. "And that pushed Winnie to come after me. I guess she thought I'd brought the law down on her." She shook her head, toying with imaginary lint on her pants. "She didn't make a lot of sense. Very irrational. And her moods were back and forth. I believe she's bipolar or has some mental illness."

"And she's the one who put the knife in Wesley's car, then called us with an anonymous tip?" Sheriff Theriot scraped the pencil against the paper.

"Yes. After she'd k-killed Jolie, she believed Wes would run back to her. When he didn't, she felt even more betrayed. That's when she decided to set him up for the murder."

Spence shook his head. "But did she call the center and ask for Jolie? To warn her?"

Felicia shook her head. "No. She says her friend called, but it was already too late."

"What about breaking in here, to your place?" the sheriff asked.

Felicia tightened her grip on Spence's hand. "She felt like I betrayed her by reporting the calls she made to the center to you. She needs psychiatric help, Sheriff."

He stood, pocketing his notebook. "We'll let the doctors decide that. Is there anything else?"

"Will she be okay? Her face, I mean?" She still couldn't believe she'd scarred someone else. Even if it was her best friend's murderer.

"I don't know. I'm heading to the hospital now." He let out a breath. "Are you sure you don't want to go to the hospital and have them check you out?"

"I'm fine, *merci.*"

"It's an obvious case of self-defense, Felicia, but I'll need you to come by the station in the morning and sign your statement." Sheriff Theriot tossed a knowing look at Spence. "Take care of her. I didn't phone Luc." He glanced back at Felicia. "That's your call to make."

Spence stood and walked the sheriff and deputy to the door. The three men spoke in hushed tones for a few moments before the door shut. Then Spence was beside her on the couch, drawing her into his arms.

She snuggled against him, finally letting the tears fall. He held her tighter, patting her back and planting feathery kisses against her forehead and temple. "Shh. It's okay. It's all over now."

"Is it?" She lifted her head and stared into his eyes. "For the rest of my life, I'll always see Winnie's face as I burned it. And I'll never forget the stench." She pinched her eyes shut, but the memory wouldn't dissipate.

"Don't do that." Spence's harsh voice snapped her eyes open. He gripped her shoulders tight. "You can't blame yourself for this."

"But I lit the lighter. I sprayed the hairspray."

"And if you hadn't, Winnie would've killed you. She'd already killed Jolie."

"I know." Her voice cracked, and she trembled. "But the flames just shot out. Her hair burned immediately."

"Don't do this, Felicia. Take it from me, you can't take the blame for this. Guilt will eat you up inside until you can't breathe. I know from experience."

"This isn't the same. I've scarred that woman for life."

"Yes, and you did what you had to in order to save your life. Self-defense. My life wasn't at stake." His fingers dug into her shoulders. "We were both dealing with murderers. Killers. People who took the lives of our loved ones. Horribly and viciously."

He spoke the truth, but she knew she wouldn't ever forget Winnie's face. "What happened to him? The guy who killed your sister?"

"He died in another bar fight while I was in prison."

She swallowed hard and stared at the floor.

Spence took her face in his gentle hands. "I won't let you allow guilt to swallow you. It will if you let it."

She stared into the depths of his eyes, registering the layers of emotions lurking there. Her throat felt as if someone had it in a vise.

Seconds ticked off the clock as he dipped his head and teased her lips with his. Her heart scrambled into overdrive. Tingles shook her hands.

He deepened the kiss, his thumbs caressing her jawline. All images of Winnie raced from her head.

Ending the kiss, Spence kept hold of her face. "I refuse to lose you. I already thought I had tonight."

Before she could reply, his lips covered hers again.

"Oh, I wish I was in the land of cotton . . ." The musical notes interrupted their embrace.

Spencer reluctantly released Felicia and snatched his cell phone from his hip.

"Old times there are not forgotten . . ." the stanza continued.

He flipped open the phone. "Yes."

"Pastor? It's Luc. I've been trying to call Felicia but keep getting her voice mail. Are you with her?"

Staring into her flushed face, Spencer's heart twisted. "Yes. I'm with her." Permanently. Even his conscience wouldn't keep him away from her any longer.

"How's she feeling? Pain medication still have her knocked out?"

Spencer covered the mouthpiece. "It's Luc. He wants to know how you're feeling."

Suspicion shot into her eyes. "The sheriff said he wouldn't tell him."

"He didn't. He's asking about your leg and the pain medication."

"Oh."

"Why don't you talk to him? Tell him what happened before he hears it from somebody else."

She hesitated, then held out her hand.

"Luc? Here she is." He passed her the phone before moving into the kitchen to give her some privacy.

Once he hit the tile around the corner, Spencer dropped to his knees.

Thank You, Father God. For Your grace and mercy, and keeping her safe. And for letting my heart know she's the one for me.

TWENTY-THREE

Spencer wiped his palms against his slacks as he smiled and nodded at the members of his congregation filing into the sanctuary. For February, it sure felt hot inside the church. He tugged at the collar cutting into his Adam's apple. Forget butterflies — nerves were sending June bugs bouncing about his gut.

The organist struck the first notes of the call to worship song, and Spencer took his place at the podium. His fingers left smear marks on the onion-paper pages of his Bible.

Lord, prepare their hearts and mine. Your will, Father, not my own.

His lips moved with the lyrics to the song, but his voice knotted before it reached his mouth. He locked gazes with the elders of the church, sitting in their regular front-left pew. Mr. Fontenot nodded and smiled. Spencer tried to smile back, but his facial muscles felt frozen.

From the front-right pew, Luc and CoCo beamed at him, but it was the woman who sat next to Luc that drew his attention. Felicia. Here to support him as he gave the most difficult sermon of his life. Her smile reached her eyes, warming him to his toes.

The past few days had been hectic, not allowing any time for the two of them to sit down and talk alone. Now that Winnie had been moved from intensive care into a regular room, she'd received a mental evaluation. They found out that Winnie suffered from bipolar disease. Had been diagnosed more than a year ago. When she was on her medication, she'd call the center and talk to Felicia. When she stopped taking her pills, she'd act on her irrational feelings. Now she was in a state hospital, where taking her medication was mandatory. Felicia had stopped wallowing in guilt and regret. The time had come to profess his love and his intentions.

But he had another confession to make first.

The last note of the song hung in the church, lingering like a bad cough after a cold. Spencer took a deep breath and gazed at Felicia.

She gave him a heartfelt smile and slight nod.

Spencer lifted his Bible and asked his congregation to join him in prayer. He asked for blessings for each member, grace and mercy for all and praised God for His guidance and love. At the "amen," every person's gaze glued on him.

He set down the Bible, silently prayed for courage and stepped out from behind the pulpit, placing a large goblet of grape juice on the stand.

"Today, I'll be referring to 1 Kings, when Solomon had built God a temple so that He might have a perpetual dwelling place. In chapter eight, Solomon dedicated the temple, praying God would forgive each person as they brought their sacrifice into the temple for the forgiveness of sins. Now, we all know that Jesus made that sacrifice for us so God could have a perpetual dwelling place in us, made clean by the sacrifice of the cross. Then He would deal with us according to our hearts and not our deeds.

"I'm going to tell you a little story this morning about God's grace and love." His gaze met Felicia's for but a minute, yet he could feel her encouragement. "Once there was a young man who lived with his mother and sister until he went off to college in another town."

He straightened his stark white shirt.

Every eye was focused on him. "He came home on weekends to help out around the house, do things for his mother and sister." He paused, praying for the courage to continue. "This particular weekend, his sister had to work late at a local fast-food restaurant. The time for her to arrive home came and went. He and his mother were worried her car had broken down, so he went to look for her."

He met Felicia's stare, saw the moisture pooling in her amazing eyes. Spencer swallowed but continued. "He arrived at her job to find the place closed down, the lights dark. Then he saw her car in the back parking lot. When he reached her vehicle, he found her dead in the back seat."

A collective gasp rose from the members of his congregation. A couple of elderly ladies pressed their fingers against their mouths.

"During the mourning process, the police arrested the man who raped and killed this young man's sister. He and his mother prepared for the trial as best they could." He locked his hands in front of him to stop the shakes. "The district attorney called his mother one day just before the trial date and informed her that due to an improper search warrant, they had to release the man they'd arrested."

Several people shuffled in the pews. Discomfort draped the members like a too-thick wool blanket on a Louisiana August night.

"But this young man found the man they'd arrested. Oh, he didn't go out looking for him, but he ran into the murderer quite by accident. The freed man said a few unwise words about the young man's sister, and the man . . . snapped."

Felicia lifted a handkerchief to her eyes. Spencer noticed CoCo and several other ladies doing the same thing. He had to continue.

"He attacked the killer. Tried to strangle him. Wanted to kill him. But he didn't. The police arrested him. He pled guilty and went to prison."

Emotions clogged his throat. Lifting the goblet, he took a big sip. He set it back on the podium, then dipped his fingers into the grape juice. Over his heart, he wiped his fingers. Purple spread over the white cotton. Even the children's stares focused on him.

"He had sin staining his heart. The sin of violence. The sin of wanting to murder. The sin of not loving others as Jesus loved the church."

He continued to dip his fingers in the goblet and smear streaks of purple across his shirt. The fabric clung to his skin, the cool dampness spreading across his chest.

"But in prison, God met the man. God put a call on his life to follow Him. The man accepted Jesus into his heart on the cold concrete floor of a twelve-by-twelve cell."

Slipping his hand into his pocket, he withdrew a small packet and tore it open. "He confessed his sins to God and asked for forgiveness."

He pulled the stain remover wet sheet free from the packet. "Now, some may say that this man in prison for a violent crime couldn't be forgiven. Couldn't be used by God. But here's the neat thing . . ." Spencer dabbed at the stain with the wet sheet. "See, God doesn't judge a man by his past actions. First Kings eight, verse thirty-nine says, *'Forgive and act; deal with each man according to all he does, since you know his heart (for you alone know the hearts of all men).'*"

The grape juice disappeared as Spencer continued to cover the area with the wet sheet. "God saw into the man's heart. Saw that he truly was sorry for his sin and repented. God saw a heart made pure again by the blood of Jesus Christ."

The stain gone, Spencer balled up the wet sheet and shoved it into his pocket. "God saw a man he could use."

He gazed over his congregation and realized he'd made his point. Now it was in God's hands.

"That man was me."

Sniffling surrounded her. Felicia glanced around. Almost all the women blotted their eyes daintily so their makeup wouldn't run. The men swallowed hard.

Spence continued his story, telling of his time in prison and the results of his first congregational confession. Members nodded as he spoke.

"I finally have learned that God forgives us the minute we ask, if we truly have repented. We don't need to punish ourselves, beat ourselves up or try for some earthly atonement."

A couple in the back said a hearty "amen."

Spence smiled. "I learned if He can use me, He can use anybody." He pointed toward the church members. "He can use every one of you, every experience you've ever had — whether you think it's bad or not, for His will."

This time, more people hollered out "amen."

Felicia thought her heart might burst, so much love and pride filled her. But also, she felt her load had been lightened by Spence's heartfelt words. She wouldn't have to carry around guilt with her for the rest of her life. All she had to do was give it to God.

As the organist moved into a popular hymn, Felicia bowed her head and left her burdens at the foot of the throne.

TWENTY-FOUR

Tangled nerves sprang in her stomach like a bungee cord.

"You look beautiful." CoCo carefully turned her to face the mirror. "Happy Fat Tuesday, Fels."

Although she'd be given clearance by her doctor to put weight on her leg, Felicia took extra care with her movements. She used her cane to balance and then met her reflection in the glass. Her breath caught. "That's m-me?"

Tara laughed, full and throaty. "Who else would it be, silly?"

The two LeBlanc sisters had definitely worked wonders.

"You have such an amazing complexion," CoCo commented as she tickled Felicia's nose with the powder brush. "I wish my skin was as fair."

"Stay out of the sun," Tara retorted.

CoCo stuck her tongue out at her little

sister and fiddled with Felicia's hair. How'd they gotten all the Mardi Gras beads to stay put in her baby-fine hair, Felicia would never know.

"Being in that airboat all day long is turning your skin to leather," Tara continued. "You're gonna look like tanned hide at your wedding."

Felicia smiled, enjoying their banter.

"Oh, put a lid on it." CoCo helped Felicia move from behind the vanity. "Let's get you into the dress. I can't wait to see it on."

"Tara, I can't thank you enough for letting me borrow it on such short notice."

The youngest LeBlanc waved away Felicia's gratitude. "I wasn't wearing it, anyway." She spun around in the room, her skirt filling as she moved. "I still can't believe I found this one on sale. It's perfect."

Felicia couldn't argue. The gold lamé clung to Tara's body before dipping into a full floor-length hem from the waist. "You are a vision, Tara LeBlanc."

Tara giggled and grabbed the dress from the hanger on the back of the bathroom door. "Let's see how this one looks on you."

The sisters gathered the full skirt and helped Felicia step inside. CoCo drew it up and secured the back. It felt as if it'd been made for Felicia. She faced the women.

"How do I look?"

"Oh, my." CoCo pressed her hand to her chest.

"What?" Felicia's heart thudded. Did it not fit? Did it look bad on her slight frame?

"You're a knockout," Tara proclaimed and moved from in front of the mirror.

Felicia couldn't breathe. The purple sequin sash draped over one shoulder, swathed to the waist. The other shoulder remained bare. Green seed pearls decorated the bodice to meet a dropped waist, then the taffeta material flowed down to a straight skirt.

"I can't believe that's me."

"Oh, you'd better believe it," Tara announced.

"Wait until your mother sees you. She'll be delighted at how stunning you are." CoCo adjusted the shoulder strap.

Felicia smiled at her friend. "I don't know how you managed to get your grandmother to pick her up for the ball, but I'm very appreciative. She'd have been hovering, and I couldn't have enjoyed my time with y'all."

CoCo squeezed her in a quick hug. "I just asked Grandmère to occupy Hattie while we got ready here. Simple." She smiled at Felicia in the mirror. "And look how scrumptious you are."

"Spence is gonna have his world rocked tonight, baby!"

"Tara, don't be crass," CoCo chastised.

"Well, he is."

A knock sounded on Felicia's bedroom door. "Ladies?"

"Just a minute," CoCo answered Luc. She grabbed her mask and affixed it over her face. Her purple satin evening gown swished as she crossed the room and opened the door.

Luc's eyes darkened with love as he stared at his bride-to-be. "Aren't you a vision of loveliness?" He planted a kiss on her temple. "I'm scared I'll muss you."

"She needs to be mussed. Anyone who has curls like that deserves being mussed up." Tara practically floated to the door. "For those of us with straight hair, it's poetic justice."

Luc laughed. "But you're looking quite beautiful as well, Tara. I'll be the envy of every man at the ball with you two beautiful ladies on my arm."

"One man will give you a run for your money in the envy-meter department." CoCo tilted her head.

"Yeah? Who?"

"Spencer Bertrand." Tara swooshed out of the way so Luc could see Felicia.

His mouth hung open. "Oh, *Boo* . . . you're so beautiful."

Heat fanned Felicia's face as she smiled. "You're my brother. Of course, you're supposed to think that."

Luc shook his head, mouth still gaping. "It's the truth. Good thing your heart's already gone, or I'd have to carry a stick to beat off all the young men tonight."

Felicia giggled. "How you do go on."

CoCo nudged her fiancé. "Close your mouth — you're gonna catch flies."

A knock sounded at the front door.

"I'll get that." Luc strode down the hall of the LeBlanc home.

"That'll be Spence." The bungee cord in Felicia's stomach sprang loose. Why was she so nervous?

CoCo laid a hand on Felicia's bare shoulder. "Don't be nervous. You're beautiful, you're going out with the man you love and you'll have a wonderful time." She helped Felicia with her mask, straightening the purple and green feathers.

Felicia gave a curt nod. CoCo squeezed her shoulder again before leaving the room.

After straightening her own mask, Tara faced Felicia. "Look, I've seen the goofy look of love on both Luc's and Jackson's faces when they were with my sisters.

Spence has the identical expression when he looks at you."

Words wouldn't form.

"He loves you, just like you love him. Stop worrying."

"I'm not so sure."

Tara cocked her eyebrow and hip. "Trust me. I know these things. Spencer Bertrand is as in love with you as Luc is with CoCo."

"Felicia?" CoCo yelled from the living room.

"Guess it's time, yes?" Felicia grabbed her cane.

"Knock his socks off, girl."

Oh, my, I'm a goner.

Spencer's heart twisted into a pretzel. Felicia glided into the room, looking so serene and beautiful, as if she belonged atop a wedding cake. His knees turned to mush.

Head down but an inch, she gazed up at him through lowered lashes. "Good evening, Spence. Happy Fat Tuesday."

This woman before him . . . this dream of purity and hope, left him speechless. He fought to form words, but cotton had taken up residence in the back of his throat.

Luc's laughter, followed by a hand clap on his shoulder, broke the moment. "Steals your breath, huh?"

Like some little boy with a crush, Spencer couldn't take his eyes off of Felicia. He nodded, not trusting himself to try to speak.

Then she smiled at him.

His world tilted on its axis. "You . . . you're beautiful. Words don't do you justice."

Pink decorated her cheeks just below the eye-area mask. "You look mighty dashing yourself, Pastor Bertrand."

He extended his arm. "Shall we?"

Her gloved hand tucked inside his elbow. Using her cane, she smiled at her brother and CoCo. "See y'all there, yes?"

"We're right behind you," Luc said.

"Tara!" CoCo yelled.

Spencer paid them no mind. All he could think about was the woman on his arm. His lady. Well, he'd sure try to make her his. Forever.

For once, the weather smiled down on Lagniappe. Stars adorned the clear sky, twinkling like glass squares on a disco ball. The full moon filled the night with light beams. Even the air felt cooler, cleaner.

He sat her in the passenger side of the truck before rushing around to slip behind the wheel. He found himself forcing to keep his focus on the road. "So, uh, what time does Luc's band play?"

"He didn't say for sure." She fiddled with the silver handle of her cane.

"That's, uh, a beautiful dress."

Her smile lit up the vehicle's cabin. "Thank you. Tara let me borrow it."

"You look much better in it than Tara ever could."

She laughed, the tinny sound causing his heart to somersault.

All too soon they parked at the community center. Ornate Mardi Gras masks hung on the double doors. Little strings of purple, green and gold lights illuminated the walkway. Spencer escorted Felicia to the door, treating her as if she was priceless.

Wasn't she?

Zydeco music squeezed into every corner of the large building. The aroma of spices from all the dishes lining the long buffet mingled together to make mouths water. Dresses swished as couples executed the Virginia reel. Every woman wore a mask — some covering their whole faces, some just between brow and cheekbone.

Spencer leaned so his mouth was at Felicia's ear. "Would you like some punch?"

She shook her head and smiled. "I'm fine now, *merci.*"

Several members of his congregation rushed forward to shake his hand in greeting. Other community members addressed him and Felicia both. The feeling of belonging nearly overwhelmed him. Finally.

Thank You, Father.

"Would you like to go out onto the veranda?"

Felicia nodded, flashing him her shy smile. He led her through the throng of people to the side French doors. The veranda's rails were decorated with strings of lights shaped like Mardi Gras masks. A nip hung in the air. Gentle breezes whispered sweet promises.

"Would you care to sit?" He pulled out one of the chairs draped in gold material.

"I'd really rather gaze out over the bayou, if you don't mind." She leaned against the rail.

His heart would explode if he didn't act. No time like the present. He sure wouldn't get a more opportune moment. Even the moon complied, reflecting off the bayou and shimmering like a teardrop solitaire. He drew in a deep breath. "Felicia, there's something I need to tell you."

She shifted ever so slightly, so that their bodies were parallel, and removed her mask. "What's wrong?"

"I'm going crazy." He took her free hand in his.

Confusion skidded across her face.

"Because I love you, *sha.*"

Her big blue eyes blinked. Once. Twice. Then they filled with moisture.

His heart sputtered, and he held her hand tighter. "I love you with everything I am, every part of me. If you'll have me, I'm yours."

Tears streaked down her face. She leaned her cane against the rail and lifted her hand to cup his face. "Oh, Spence."

His heart threatened to pound right out of his chest. He lowered his head and kissed her. Softly, gently. He wound their joined hands between them as he kissed her with all the love in his heart.

She broke off the kiss.

Spencer froze. Did she not want his love? Maybe he shouldn't have just blurted out his feelings without having talked with her first. Doubts circled his heart like a gator after a crane.

"Do you know how long I've wanted to hear you say that?" Her voice quivered. "How I've prayed you'd say those words to me? But never in my dreams was it put as poetically as you just did."

Hope flared in his chest.

"Spence, I love you with everything I am, every part of me." She sniffed. "If you'll have me, I'm yours."

He could almost hear his heart singing. His words, her voice . . . He wrapped his arms around her and pulled her in for another kiss.

A kiss that'd last a lifetime.

EPILOGUE

April

Could someone explode from pure happiness? Felicia didn't know for sure, but if it were possible, she'd be a prime candidate.

The spring breeze danced across the backyard of the Trahan home, carrying the sweet scent of azalea and honeysuckle on its wings. The sun had already begun its descent and soon would melt behind the tree line of the bayou. Crickets and cicadas chirped in harmony.

Beautiful bouquets of magnolia blossoms draped from the end chair on each row, fastened with white satin ribbons. A white runner down the middle of the rows boasted a trim of gold on the edges. At the end of the runner stood a gazebo, especially constructed for this happy event. White latticework covered the back, and English ivy had been threaded throughout the intricate design. Large boughs of magnolia blooms and leaves decorated the top of the arch.

Felicia stared out the window as people took their seats in the white chairs. She gripped the handle of the flower bouquet and turned to face the women in the room.

Tara, looking absolutely breathtaking in the yellow dress that perfectly contrasted with her tanned skin, lifted a veil. Alyssa, who had recently eloped with Jackson Devereaux, looked positively radiant in her matching yellow dress. She helped her younger sister settle the veil with pouffy netting on CoCo's crown.

Mrs. LeBlanc mopped at her eyes. "You look so much like Mother LeBlanc, your *grand-père's* mother."

Sitting at a brass vanity, CoCo smiled at her grandmother through the mirror.

The older woman planted a whisper of a kiss against CoCo's cheek. "You're darling, *ma chérie.* I wish your parents could be here."

CoCo grabbed her grandmother's hand. "In my heart, they *are* here."

Mrs. LeBlanc patted CoCo's shoulder before heading to the door. "Time for me to take my place. I'll see you outside."

Felicia lifted the hem of her own sunshine dress and stood behind the LeBlanc sisters. Her eyes met CoCo's in the reflection. "I just wanted to tell you now, before it all gets hectic, how incredibly happy I am to have you as a sister." She blinked back tears and included Alyssa and Tara in her warm gaze. "And I thank you both for sharing this wonderful woman with me and my family."

CoCo joined her grandmother in blotting her eyes while fanning herself with her hands. "Oh, shush now. You're gonna make me cry and make a big mess of my makeup. What'll your brother think if I walk down the aisle looking like I have two black eyes?"

Tara and Alyssa laughed, but not Felicia. She dabbed at her own tears. "He'll think he's the luckiest man in Lagniappe. And he'll be right."

CoCo stood and moved from the vanity. She gave Felicia a side hug, then pulled her sisters into the embrace. "I'm so blessed to have each of you in my life."

Each woman hugged tighter. No words were said. None were needed.

A knock rapped against the door. "Everybody decent?"

Tara replied with an "as decent as we can be" before Jackson stuck his head inside. "Hey, ladies. It's about time to get this show on the road."

Alyssa scooted her new husband out the door. "Give us a second. We'll be out in just a minute."

He waggled his eyebrows at his bride. "Sixty seconds, and if you aren't out in the hall lining up, I'm coming in after y'all."

She laughed and planted a kiss on his mouth before shutting the door. "Okay, let's do this." She grabbed the large bouquet of white roses and handed them to CoCo. "We'll be right in front of you. This is it, the moment you've waited for all your life."

"Haven't we all?" Tara groaned. "Finally, *Grand-mère* and I will have the house to ourselves."

Her dry humor broke the serious moment, and all of them laughed. CoCo drew a deep breath and smiled, joy radiating from her face. "I'm so ready."

They moved into the hall where Jackson leaned against the wall, looking nonchalant and very debonair in his black tuxedo with tails. Tara headed through the French doors first, her spine straight as she walked. Felicia gave CoCo a quick air kiss, careful not to muss the veil, then followed Tara down the white runner. She could make out Alyssa's footfalls behind her.

Felicia smiled at the townsfolk of Lagniappe as she walked. Tara had taken white ribbon and tied a bow with a magnolia bloom to the cane. Felicia felt like a princess. She nodded at her mother in the front row. Hattie's perfect face was already stained with tears.

Then, Felicia looked up to the gazebo.

Her brother stood in a white tuxedo, the love on his face matching what she'd seen moments ago. Beside him stood Bubba Theriot, his best man, in a black tuxedo. He looked quite dashing without his glasses and had gotten his red hair cut into a buzz.

But it was the man in the middle, wearing a white collar and holding a Bible, that set Felicia's pulse afire.

Pastor Spencer Bertrand stood solemnly in the center of the gazebo. His shaggy hair had also been trimmed into a shorter cut. The result made his eyes stand out more and made his strong jaw more prominent. His bright smile caught the setting sun's last rays. His gaze latched onto Felicia's as she took her place alongside Tara. He winked — her heart flipped in response.

Alyssa joined her and Tara on the edge of the gazebo. Luc's zydeco band started on cue. The guests stood and faced the French doors just as Jackson escorted CoCo down the aisle.

Felicia thought her heart would break from the sight of sheer elation beaming from CoCo. The bride's stare never left her groom's. When Jackson and CoCo stopped at the gazebo, the guests sat.

"Who gives this woman in holy matrimony?" Spence asked, his voice calm.

"Her family does," replied Jackson. He slowly lifted the veil from her face, draping it over her head, and gave her a small kiss on the cheek. "You go, sis," he whispered just loud enough for the wedding party to hear before moving to stand on the other side of Bubba.

Felicia turned in unison with Alyssa and Tara to face Spence as Luc took CoCo's hand.

Spence flashed Felicia a quick smile. "Today, we celebrate not only the joining of this man and woman before God, but also the joining of these two families in love and in honor of CoCo and Luc."

Warm tears spread over Felicia's cheeks, but she didn't care. The desires of her heart were satisfied on this glorious dusk. She was acquiring not only the sister she'd always wanted, but two others as well. Her brother's state could only be described as ecstatic. Her mother was set on the road to a full recovery from her drinking crutch. And the man she loved, well, he loved her too.

But the most amazing aspect of Felicia's happiness was the knowledge that God loved her. No more guilt and condemnation, only grace and love.

She closed her eyes as Luc recited his vows.

Thank you, God, for this day. For these people. For the love You've shown us through these connections.

Spence pronounced CoCo and Luc man and wife just as the last purple streaks of the sun disappeared over the bayou. Felicia cried tears of joy from her heart as Spence introduced Mr. and Mrs. Luc Trahan to the guests. The crowd of well-wishers exploded in applause.

Felicia caught Spence's attention. He winked and mouthed *I love you.*

Her heart fluttered and she mouthed the words back.

God was very good, indeed.

Dear Reader,

Welcome back to Cajun country! South Louisiana has such a wonderful and diverse culture, even different from other southern states. With its richness and vibrancy, the bayou has been the perfect backdrop for this series.

I've loved writing about the people of Lagniappe with all their struggles, and I thank you for journeying with me.

I based the character of Felicia loosely on my niece, Krystina. Her most positive outlook on life and strong faith has been an inspiration to me. I hope Felicia's story will encourage and uplift you.

I love hearing from readers. Please visit me at www.robincaroll.com and drop me a line, or write to me at PO Box 242091, Little Rock, AR, 72223. Join my newsletter group . . . sign my guest book. I look forward to hearing from you.

Blessings,
Robin Caroll

QUESTIONS FOR DISCUSSION

1. Felicia was born with a handicap that kept her from certain physical activities, yet she never blamed God. Have you ever dealt with an injury or handicap? Did you blame God? How did you endure your trials?

2. Spencer had a past that he regretted. Have you ever hidden something from your past to avoid embarrassment? What did you do when the truth came out?

3. Felicia's brother was overprotective of her, out of love, and it annoyed her. Has someone who cared for you ever been overbearing? How did you respond?

4. Spencer had to learn that everything, including his congregation's reaction to his past, was in God's hands. How do you deal with the difficulty of placing some-

thing that could affect your future totally in God's hands?

5. Winnie acted on her jealous emotions. Have you ever reacted out of envy? How did you feel later?

6. Wesley was falsely imprisoned. Have you ever believed the worst about someone, only to find out later you were wrong? What did you do?

7. Felicia wanted to be independent, but she needed to learn that we aren't made to be independent of God. How do you deal with your independent streak while leaning on God?

8. Spencer didn't believe he was worthy of doing good things, yet God had a different plan for him. Have you ever thought you were destined for something, only to have God steer you in a different direction? How did you handle the situation?

9. Felicia and Spencer had to learn to release guilt and pain over the past to move forward in their relationship. Has something from your past ever caused your current relationships to suffer? How

did you react?

10. Even though she acted in self-defense, Felicia felt guilty over harming Winnie. Have you ever been put in a situation where you had to defend yourself? How did you feel?

11. Felicia's past was riddled with pain and disappointment. Have you ever felt like that? How did you manage?

12. Before Spencer turned to God, he acted in ways that he wasn't proud of. Before you became born again, how did you act? How did you change?

13. Felicia felt as if she owed it to her friend, Jolie, to bring the murderer to justice. Have you ever felt you had a "debt" to someone? What did you do?

14. Felicia was surrounded with family and friends who loved her. Many would consider her blessed, despite her handicap. How can we be loving and supportive of those we cherish?

ABOUT THE AUTHOR

Born and raised in Louisiana, **Robin Car-oll** is a Southern belle right down to her "hey y'all." Her passion has always been to tell stories to entertain others. Robin's mother, bless her heart, is a genealogist who instilled in Robin the deep love of family and pride of heritage — two aspects Robin weaves into each of her books. When she isn't writing, Robin spends time with her husband of eighteen years, her three beautiful daughters and their four character-filled cats at home — in the South, where else? An avid reader herself, Robin loves hearing from and chatting with other readers. Although her favorite genre to read is mystery/suspense, of course, she'll read just about any good story. Except historicals! To learn more about this author of deep South mysteries of suspense to inspire your heart, visit Robin's Web site at www.robin caroll.com.

The employees of Thorndike Press hope you have enjoyed this Large Print book. All our Thorndike, Wheeler, and Kennebec Large Print titles are designed for easy reading, and all our books are made to last. Other Thorndike Press Large Print books are available at your library, through selected bookstores, or directly from us.

For information about titles, please call:
(800) 223-1244

or visit our Web site at:
http://gale.cengage.com/thorndike

To share your comments, please write:
Publisher
Thorndike Press
295 Kennedy Memorial Drive
Waterville, ME 04901